I0671386

Chesapeake Bay Christmas

Volume III

JM Johansen
Julie Leverenz
Narielle Living
Gloria Savage-Early

High Tide Publications, Inc.
Deltaville, Virginia

Copyright © 2014 by JM Johansen, Julie Leverenz, Narielle Living and Gloria Savage-Early.

Edited by Narielle Living (NarielleLiving.com)
Photography by Julie Leverenz (JulieLeverenz.com)

All rights reserved. No part of this publication may be reproduced, distributed or transmitted in any form or by any means, including photocopying, recording, or other electronic or mechanical methods, without the prior written permission of the publisher, except in the case of brief quotations embodied in critical reviews and certain other noncommercial uses permitted by copyright law. For permission requests, write to the publisher, addressed "Attention: Permissions Coordinator," at the address below.

High Tide Publications
1000 Bland Point Road
Deltaville, Virginia 23043
HighTidePublications.com

Publisher's Note: This is a work of fiction. Names, characters, places, and incidents are a product of the author's imagination. Locales and public names are sometimes used for atmospheric purposes. Any resemblance to actual people, living or dead, or to businesses, companies, events, institutions, or locales is completely coincidental.

Chesapeake Bay Christmas, Volume III/ Johansen, Leverenz, Living, Savage-Early -- 1st edition.
ISBN 978-0988463738

Table of Contents

I'll be Home for Christmas

JM Johansen

For Linda Tiller

Chapter 1

"I can't believe you're putting up that damn Christmas tree again this year. It's just the two of us."

Nonie Roberts stopped hanging the ornament she held in her hand. She stood quietly for a moment, clearly trying to calm herself. It was too late for composure; he saw the heat rising in her neck. She turned slowly to face her husband of forty-five years. "Harley, I wish you would leave me alone."

Harley considered his options. He knew from his experience over the last fifteen years that he could either be right or be at peace. He decided to be right.

"Damn it, Nonie. He isn't coming home. He didn't come home last year, the year before that, or the year before that. What in hell's name makes you think this year will be any different?"

With that outburst from her husband, Nonie turned her back to Harley. Her shoulders began to shake, quietly at first then more violently with each passing minute. *Oh, Jeez. It's gonna be a long night.* He stood up from his recliner in the corner and walked across the den to Nonie. He put his arms around her heaving shoulders to try to comfort her. She brushed him off and turned to face him.

"You're a jackass, Harley. Leave me be. For God's sake, this is my tradition. I do it every year, have done it every year, and will continue to do it every year. It doesn't involve you. You don't help, you don't clean up, you don't do nothing. So leave me the hell alone."

"He was my son too," Harley countered.

"He *is* my son, Harley. Not was. Not past tense. *Is!* Now, leave me in peace."

Harley saw he had lost the battle. He shrugged. "Guess I'll turn in then. Enjoy yourself." He attempted to give his wife a kiss, but from the murderous expression in her eyes, he thought better of it.

"'Night, Nonie," he said as he walked down the hall to the bedroom. He climbed into the king-size bed and pulled the covers up to his chin. He tried to remember the last time he and Nonie shared the same bed. He couldn't dredge it up. Within five minutes he was asleep.

*****

As soon as she heard the door to the master bedroom shut, Nonie reached into the bottom of the Christmas tree ornament box and pulled out a small green photo album. She lowered herself slowly to the loveseat next to the tree. Arthritis and years of being on her feet at the grocery store had ruined her back. She remembered being a young girl, dancing and climbing trees. *If I was to climb one now they'd have to get the cherry picker to get me down.* She snickered at the thought of the volunteer fire department coming to rescue her. *God, would I be the talk of the town!*

Putting the album on her lap, she began the annual ritual of studying the pictures inside. The first picture was Davey just after he enlisted. He looked so smart in his tie and long sleeved white shirt. His dad made him dress up in his church clothes. "This is a very important occasion, Davey," Harley told him, his hands on his son's shoulders. "You're joining the Marines, just like I did. I'm proud of you, son." That in itself was a rarity. Harley was always slow with the compliments and generous with the criticism.

Nonie stared at the picture, concentrating on Davey's eyes. *The eyes are the window to the soul.* That's what her mama always told her. He was such a handsome boy, even if he was his own. He had so much promise.

Coming up, he worked at the family grocery store. Tibbons Grocery had been in her family for four generations, all the way back to the Civil War. She and Harley had worked side by side in their younger days. "That boy has eyes on you," her mama told her. "More like eyes on your inheritance," her daddy would counter. "He can have my inheritance," Nonie would say, her cheeks burning with the thought of Harley Roberts.

Harley had started working at the grocery when he was thirteen. His daddy had died, and he was helping his mother raise his two younger brothers. He stayed in school, coming in after his classes. When he graduated high school in Middlesex County, Nonie's daddy gave him three hundred dollars as a graduation present. "This is for you, Harley. Spend it on yourself, or save it as you will. You're a good boy!"

Shortly after that, Harley enlisted in the Marine Corps in January 1945. He was sent to the Pacific and came back a hero after the war ended later that year. All the girls were after him, but he only had eyes for Nonie. On New Year's Eve he proposed and Nonie turned him down.

Her father was furious. "You don't exactly have them lining up outside the grocery for your hand in marriage, Nonie! This man is a war hero."

"He isn't a war hero. He is a Marine that was in the Pacific. Besides, after I graduate in June I think I might go on to college. Why don't you pass the grocery on to Harley?"

Had her mother not intervened, Nonie's dad would have hit her. "Nonie," her mother had said, a hint of sorrow in her voice disguised as concern, "we don't have the money to send you to college."

"I've been saving my wages, and Mr. Mann says he'll help me get a scholarship. I could work at the college to earn my keep. I really want to go, Mama. Please."

"Well, you'll be eighteen in March and then there isn't a damn thing we can do about it. What an ungrateful daughter you are, Nonie. I am so disappointed in you," her father retorted as he turned back to stocking shelves.

Now, it was not Harley Roberts' nature to give up easily. He went back to work at the grocery after he had been discharged from the Marines. He would joke with Nonie's father, make Nonie's mama laugh with his jokes and impersonations of Winston Churchill. Occasionally he'd even get Nonie to crack a smile.

On Nonie's birthday, Harley brought in a dozen roses in a beautiful milk glass vase. They were blood red with baby's breath and ferns. He had carried them from the parking lot into the store. A couple of the old ladies in town stopped to admire them. "Oh, Harley! Are those for me?" Harley just shook his head no.

He took them into the store that morning. It was his day off, but he came in anyway to see Nonie on her birthday. When Nonie, who had been dusting shelves with her feather duster, turned around, there stood Harley with the roses.

"I wanted to come in and wish you a happy birthday. I'd like to take you to dinner tonight if you'll agree."

She did agree. That night, dressed in one of her mama's nicer church dresses, they went to The River's Inn. "This is an expensive place, Harley," Nonie said, astonished that he would take her to such a place.

"You're worth it. I thought we could have a nice dinner for your birthday. I just wanted—"

She cut him off mid-sentence. "Harley, I don't want you to get any wrong ideas here. I like you, but I want to go to college after high school. I don't want to work in the grocery for the rest of my life like my mama and her mama before her."

"Nonie, I am just taking you out for your birthday. No strings attached."

They talked that night. Harley said he wanted to stay in Deltaville, maybe manage the store for her dad after he got too old to do it. He didn't expect anything from her father; he just loved Deltaville and after his experience in the Pacific he didn't want to go anywhere else.

"Don't you want to see the world?" Nonie asked.

"I've seen enough of the world—all I want to. I couldn't wait to get back home. Let me tell you, the world isn't all it's cracked up to be. After you see someone die in a war, it all changes."

Nonie nodded. "Well, I told my dad I didn't want the grocery, to give it to you because he thinks of you like the son he didn't have. He needs to heap his dreams on someone besides me. I really want to go to college."

"Where?" Harley asked.

"Mary Baldwin up in Staunton. I can work and go to school. I really want to be a writer, Harley. Can you understand?"

Harley was quiet. He seemed to be studying his hands and the napkin in them as if he had never seen anything like it.

"Nonie, I love you. I want you to be happy. Let's do this. Let's get engaged and after you graduate in June we'll get married. Then you can go up to Staunton in September and start school and you won't have to work. I'll work and pay for your school. You could come home on the weekends or I'll come up there."

Nonie looked at him, maybe for the first time. He wasn't the bumbling boy three years her senior who worked in the grocery. He was a man who wanted to share his life and dreams with her.

"Yes, Harley. I'll marry you under the condition that I get to go to school in September."

He pulled the ring from his pocket and handed it to her. "Thank you! You have made me so happy."

They went back to Nonie's home and told her parents. "I'm going to go on to college in Staunton in September," Nonie told both of them. Harley shot her dad a knowing look, and Mr. Tibbons winked at him.

They were married on June 10, 1948, and two months later Nonie learned she was pregnant with Davey. Thus ended her hopes of college.

From the minute she learned she was pregnant, she was determined the child she was carrying wouldn't meet the same fate. Every month, she put money away in the Kotex box under the sink in the bathroom so her child could go off to college. She didn't want her baby to have to work in the family grocery store.

She knew Harley would never look in a Kotex box. The thought of it made her laugh out loud. When the box filled up, she would drive all the way to Kilmarnock to put the money in the savings account she had set up at the Community Bank. She didn't dare use the bank in Deltaville; there were no secrets in her hometown.

She turned the page. There he was, her Davey! He was holding flowers for his sweetheart Missy; his Marine Corps haircut made him look so much younger. He had on his green uniform, she remembered the pride, and dread she felt that day in 1967. He was going to Viet Nam.

Facing that picture was the one of Missy and Davey at the altar in the Methodist church in Deltaville. Pastor Marking stood behind them in his robe and vestments. He had just married her son and Missy. They had decided not to wait until he got back. Missy was going on the train with him to Parris Island in North Carolina where they had a hotel room booked for three days before he had to report for duty and deployment to Viet Nam.

They weren't sure they were getting married at first. Nonie remembered the anguish Davey had gone through to get his commanding officer's permission. Finally, the commanding officer relented, and Davey could keep his promise to his beloved Missy.

The next three or four pages held pictures of Davey with Nonie, Davey with his father, and Davey with his fellow Marines. She spent a long time staring at the next picture of Davey and Missy boarding the train in Richmond for their North Carolina destination. Harley tried to pretend he wasn't crying, but she had seen the tears rolling down his cheeks just before he wiped them off. "Just sweating," he mumbled when Nonie tried to comfort him.

She knew he wasn't sweating. It was November and thirty-eight degrees. They drove back to Deltaville in silence.

Except for the last two pictures in the album, the rest were photos of Davey in Viet Nam. Bare-chested Davey; Davey with, his arm around another Marine; Davey sleeping; Davey eating; Davey in the fields, in rice patties, in the truck he drove.

After seven months in Viet Nam, he and Missy got together in Hawaii. They called it R&R—short for rest and recuperation. They stayed at the Hilton Rainbow Towers on Waikiki. He called home. Nonie had answered the ringing telephone and she remembered the sound of her son's voice on the other end. It was a break from the fighting. It was the beginning of their life together because Missy got pregnant on that trip.

Davey had signed up for thirteen months. Even though he was only required to serve for six months, the incentives the Marines offered changed his mind. Nonie was never sure why he decided to serve a third tour; he claimed it was because if you were willing to extend your tour an additional six months, they would give you a free leave of thirty days in between the two tours, flying you anywhere you wanted to spend it free of charge. "The flight time doesn't count toward those thirty days, and I can take Missy somewhere nice before the baby is born."

Harley didn't understand it either because in World War II you served until the war was over. He shook his head when Nonie related to him that Marine battalion was permanently based in-country, and individual soldiers were rotated in and out of country to and from that unit.

When he came home during the thirty days leave, Nonie realized that her son had changed. He was no longer the easy, carefree boy she knew. She kept her granddaughter because the crying upset Davey. Missy said he would wake up in the middle of the night screaming. Once she had tried to comfort him, and he hit her hard enough to bounce her off the bed.

By the end of his thirty day leave, things were improving. Missy held out hope that when she got her husband back, things would return to normal.

The news came right before Christmas. Davey had been wounded while fighting in the Mekong Delta. He was in San Diego at the Naval Hospital. Nonie wanted to go with Missy, but her daughter-in-law wanted to spare her. One of Davey's friends had said it was bad. He was right.

She closed the album. She wasn't ready to look at the last five pages.

Chapter 2

The Tupperware container rested uncomfortably in Sarge's icy hands. He had given his last pair of gloves away, so his exposed fingers resembled mottled blue sausages. It was the third Tuesday in December, and the weather was freezing. The cold and damp dug deep into his bones this morning as he waited for the Veteran's Center to open at 0700 hours.

Buzz was waking up next to him after a tough round of nightmares fighting the Viet Cong in his restless dreams. . He had roused Sarge from a deep sleep somewhere around 0200 hours by standing over him, swaying back and forth like a deranged rocking horse. Sarge's quick blow to his right leg sent Buzz to his knees and back to reality. The rest of the night was peaceful.

"What time is it, Sarge?" Buzz asked.

"Fifteen more minutes 'til she opens up," Sarge answered. "Don't ask me again. And don't ask me if we're there yet."

It was their little joke. Sarge's son used to ask that all the time from the back seat of the car. "We'll get there when we get there, son," he'd say. It was a bittersweet memory.

"Papa Smurf ain't doin' so good this morning. His eyes look glassy," Buzz managed to croak. Once Buzz had his coffee, he sounded better. Sleeping on the street can leave your mouth tasting like it was full of wet sawdust. Sarge wanted to remind him Papa Smurf had a glass eye. He thought better of it.

"Put him toward the middle so he'll stay warm. Can't do much else 'til she opens up."

They moved the Viet Nam veteran they called Papa Smurf to the inside. No one asked the time again. Time was meaningless for homeless warriors living on the street. And no one asked if they were at their destination, or even close to it. They all knew there was no stop beyond this one.

The wait was easier on some mornings, especially if the weather was obliging. Today wasn't one of those days. The group of twenty or so huddled together on the streets of Richmond, Virginia, not far from the Marine Corps recruiting station. They ranged in age from seventy to twenty-one. All damaged goods. All veterans. All homeless. The cold wind lashed them as it zipped around the corner, causing them to pull in tighter.

"Any minute now. Any minute now," Buzz mumbled under his breath. No one seemed to listen except Papa Smurf.

Sarge hated it when one of them died on the street. It meant the cops would come and roust them from their sanctuary. It meant he had to hide the Tupperware so they wouldn't take it away. It meant questions with no answers. "How long did you know him? Any family? What's his name? What's your name? Where do you live?"

The cops always thought the group was being evasive. It wasn't that they didn't know the answers. They just weren't telling.

The lights were on in the center now and between that and the sun peeking over the roof of the building spirits started to improve. Buzz and Sarge helped Papa Smurf to his feet. "Let's get you inside, Papa Smurf," Sarge muttered as the two staggered under the dead weight of the soldier's body. Papa Smurf had been on the streets for forty-five years and he had always kept his white beard and hair trimmed no matter what. This morning they were matted with dirt and his skin was the color of an overripe banana.

"What do ya think?" Buzz mumbled to no one in particular.

"Don't look good," Sarge countered.

Chapter 3

Nonie finished decorating the Christmas tree at two a.m. She had everything on it except the special ornament and the angel that went on the top. Davey had always waited to put the little green elf on the tree. He had made it in a first-grade art class, and each year they would unwrap it from the piece of velvet and he would place it on the tree. Then Davey would climb the stepladder and put the angel on top. "Now it's finished," Nonie would say.

"Ain't it beautiful, mama? Ain't it beautiful?"

"Yes, Davey. It's beautiful...the most beautiful tree in all the world."

Missy would be coming over later with Davey's two children. She always left the girl from her second marriage at home with her husband. Missy was a kind girl, and Davey's two girls were nineteen and fifteen. *This might be the last year they come. No one wants to visit with an old lady who talks about a man they barely knew.*

Nonie cleaned up the mess and took the boxes down to the basement. She pulled the photo album from one of the dusty bookcases and carried it to the guest room where she had taken up residence. She didn't want to look at the last three pictures tonight. "I've got to get my rest," she said to no one in particular. "They'll be here in nine hours."

She drifted off to sleep, the photo album clutched tightly to her chest.

Chapter 4

Sarge nodded in acknowledgement and eased his six foot, thirty-eight year old body into one of the chairs in the small room. He had sat watch too many times lately, and the weariness of holding these guys hands as they passed on was getting to him in ways he never dreamed possible. He'd seen a lot of it on the battlefield where it was expected. All of them thought the war would be over when they got home. For some it was. Not for him, or Buzz, or Papa Smurf. It would never be over for them until they died.

"You can go on if you'd like," a voice behind him crooned. "This old man's dying. Nothing you can do here." He ignored the voice in his head, gripping Papa Smurf's hand even tighter.

"You think he'd let you hold his hand if he knew what was in that Tupperware dish you carry around? You think any of these men would call you 'leader' if they knew?"

Sarge held both the hand of his companion and the Tupperware container even tighter as the voice serenaded them both. It did no good to tell his tormentor to stop. He'd been trying to get it to stop for ten years and it was a hopeless cause.

He must have dozed off. He was home again and it was warm and the breeze off the Chesapeake was calming. His wife was with him and his son, barely ten years old, was running toward him, fishing poles clutched in both hands. He could hear the gulls and feel the sun and all was well. No war. No closed head injury. No homelessness on the streets of Richmond.

All was well. That's how he knew it was a dream.

*****

"Sarge! Sarge!" He heard his name called, but sleep wouldn't release him easily. Now someone was shaking him hard and calling his name louder and louder.

He opened one eye. "What?"

It was Buzz. "Sarge, they took Papa Smurf to the hospital."

Sarge bolted upright. Where was his Tupperware?

"You dropped this." Buzz said. He handed him the Tupperware container he had retrieved from under the chair.

Sarge tried hard not to snatch it from Buzz, but he couldn't help himself. "Thanks," he mumbled.

"What's in that thing, anyway?"

"You don't want to know."

"Hey, Papa Smurf is in bad shape. The cops just talked to me and want you soon as you wake up and can talk. They're in the next room."

Sarge panicked. Usually he was on the street when they came along with their notebooks and questions. He could hide the

Tupperware safely in several spots he had claimed for just such emergencies. No hiding it now. Not in here.

He looked toward the door. It was blocked by the bulk of two detectives. He recognized one of them — a man who had been in his unit in Baghdad. He didn't fear recognition anymore — living on the streets had changed his appearance to the point that he didn't recognize his own face in the mirror of the bathroom.

"Buzz, listen. I need you to take this and keep it 'til I'm finished. Don't open it. I'm trusting you here."

It was the only time it had been out of his control in the five years he had been carrying it around.

"You can trust me, Sarge. I'll sit right here with it 'til you're done."

Nodding, Sarge went out to face the two detectives. He answered their questions as best he wanted to, then went back to fetch his Tupperware from Buzz. Sarge found him on a gurney, fast asleep, clutching the container to his chest. Buzz was a man you could count on. He shook Buzz gently and then backed up. Sometimes when you wake a man up he'll knock you silly. Reflex and war did that to a person.

Chapter 5

Nonie jolted upright in bed. It was already nine a.m. and she had to shower, dress, and fix the Christmas cookies before Missy and the girls arrived. She knew Harley would be of no use; he had tried to bond with his granddaughters, but they both favored Davey. Now he sat in his recliner when they came to visit and pretended to be asleep.

Missy and the girls arrived just as she pulled the last baking sheet of cookies from the oven. Every time they came she marveled at the change in them, especially Gabby , the youngest. She looked so much like Davey, and as she matured, it was even more so. To think—if Missy hadn't woken up all those years ago, she'd be dead. The thought sent a bolt of lightning shiver down Nonie's spine.

Over the past fourteen years, Nonie had tried everything to find Davey. After he left the VA hospital in Richmond, he had come back to Deltaville. The shame of the "Christmas Eve Incident", as the people of Deltaville liked to call it, was too much for him. One morning he was just gone. Forever gone.

Harley blamed himself. "I'm the one who wanted him to enlist—even though he could have had a deferment. I'm the one who told him to 'man up' the day he left. I thought he was being a pussy. "

"You didn't know, Harley," Nonie had told him a million times if she told him once.

"I was wrong, Nonie. I thought there was nothing wrong with him."

"They didn't know about post-traumatic stress disorder until several years later."

"Is that what they call it now? We called it 'shell shock' or 'battle fatigue'. Who knew?"

Nonie had emptied the saving account from the Kotex box in the ensuing years. She hired private detectives, subscribed to the Virginia and North Carolina newspapers, and searched daily for unidentified men her son's age. Posters and rewards covered telephone poles in every major city. Fifteen years later—nothing.

Maybe it's just as well, Nonie thought. The people here would never forget what happened or let Davey forget it, for that matter.

Chapter 6

Every month more and more of them were rousted from their sleep and told to move on. The abandoned buildings had been boarded up, and space was becoming scarce. An upside to this was they had to huddle closer together in the alleyways that were still available to them. They kept warm that way.

Some of the cops were ex-military. They would look the other way, or move them to an area that hadn't been touched by the developers. They also told their fellow officers to lay off. A couple of them recognized Sarge as one of the medics that had tended to their buddies. Often they'd slip him a burger for dinner in gratitude. He'd split it into pieces and give it to his men.

Tonight none of the cops were the good guys. They were all told to move on and they did, marching off to a safe spot three blocks over.

Sarge hated this spot.

*****

In Narcotics Anonymous, there is a saying that the program is a gateway to strength and hope. After getting back from Baghdad, Sarge had entered the gateway. He never found strength or hope. He knew then he was a terminal addict.

He had invisible wounds. One of them was his addiction to narcotics, and one of them was a closed head injury that went undiagnosed during his two tours in Iraq.

He came home to his wife Veronica and his two daughters— home to the only things that had kept him going in Baghdad. An IED had blown him from his vehicle. The doctor said he was fine and lucky and sent him back to care for the "real victims of this war," the doc had told him unsympathetically. "The ones missing legs and arms. Stop whining, Sargent. You are lucky. These men are not."

He had returned to the U.S. facing a hero's welcome. He was back with his wife and his girls, and he knew he was not the same.

So did Veronica.

He tried everything to reintegrate himself into the community. His skills as a medic landed him a job in the local hospital, but his irritability and failure to recall conversations, difficult concentrating and inability to make decisions caused his superiors to fire him. They had given him a neutral reference, but the staff nurses knew he had been taking extra drugs from the locked cabinet at the nurses' station room and charging them to patients.

After experiencing his mood swings and outbursts, Veronica had fired him from their marriage also. He got to see the girls under supervised visitation, but that failed too, and so he headed for the streets and the companionship of other veterans who knew his pain and asked no questions.

Except about the Tupperware.

Chapter 7

Later that afternoon, after Missy and the girls left and Nonie finished cleaning the kitchen, she walked outside to the back desk. You could see the lights from the small town of Mathews across the river reflected like stars on the water. The night was so peaceful, so quiet, so cold—just like it was fifteen years ago. She wrapped the blanket she had taken from the linen closet around her, and sat on the green Adirondack chair. She hadn't taken that one into the shed for some reason.

The cold air and the clear night sky and the peaceful river took her back fifteen years.

Missy and Davey and the girls were down here, right here at this point on the river. They had been fishing, even though it was Thanksgiving Day. I remember how cold they were. That was fifteen years ago; no, it couldn't be. My mama always said the older you get the quicker time goes. My God, Gabby is sixteen now, and Bella nineteen.

Oh, yes. We were all going to bed because we were exhausted. Missy and Davey and the girls were upstairs in Davey's old room.

We had warmed them up with hot chocolate and marshmallows and they were nodding off. I remember Harley carrying Bella upstairs. She was wearing that red flannel nightgown we bought for her.

Harley came back down. We were sitting in the sunroom and he reached over and patted my knee. "Time to go to bed, old girl." He always called me old girl, even when I was younger and prettier and my boobs didn't sag.

We got changed for bed and I remember looking at the clock just before I drifted off. It was 11:45.

The next thing was the banging and the screaming. Missy was banging on our door hard as she could. I jumped up and ran and opened the door. She was screaming like people do when someone dies. Bella was hold on to her momma's leg and she was hysterical crying. I grabbed her and shook her and kept saying "What is it? What happened?"

Harley was right behind me and he finally slapped Missy right across her face. It musta startled her because she stopped crying long enough to tell us that Davey had Gabby down at the river and was trying to drown her.

"You must have been having some sort a nightmare," Harley had said. But he put on his big heavy bathrobe anyway.

Missy said, "It isn't a nightmare. I went downstairs with Gabby because she was hungry and I didn't want to wake up Davey so I fed her down there. Then I went back up and put her in the bed with us so she'd go to sleep. About twenty minutes later, I heard Davey. I thought he was getting up to use the bathroom. But no, he was talking crazy, like he was back in Viet Nam. He grabbed Gabby up off the bed and ran out the house fast as he could and I ran after him and he went right straight for the river."

Oh, God! The baby. Nonie was the first to reach Davey. He held Gabby in his outstretched hands and over and over dunked her into the freezing river.

Nonie grabbed his arm, but he threw her backwards and she landed on the frozen sand. She cried out for him to stop. "She's on fire. She's on fire." Davey kept repeating the words over and over.

It took Missy and Harley to restrain him. He had placed Gabby in the river. Nonie ran and plucked her out. She stripped off her bathrobe and wrapped her granddaughter in its warmth, all the time running back to the house.

Davey had stopped struggling and was holding on to his wife. "I thought it was the baby with the Napalm. I thought she was on fire."

The following day I drove him to Richmond. He checked himself in to the psych unit at the Veterans Hospital and stayed there for nine months. Missy stood by him the whole time, even though folks urged her to divorce him while he was in the hospital. She was the only one who believed he was going to get better. Nonie knew from the look in his eyes he wasn't going to be Davey again anytime soon.

He came back home a shell of himself. They had done some shock treatments on him. Of course, Harley had him working in the grocery. But it was a small grocery in a small, mean town and people would talk behind their hands when they came in. Mothers would grab their children in their arms when he approached.

Nonie never knew for sure what triggered him to pack his bags that Sunday morning, but when she went upstairs to tell him breakfast was ready, his duffle bag was gone. The note on his bed said he was leaving, for Missy to divorce him and get on with her life. "I'd kill myself, but I don't have the guts. I'm sorry, mama. I love you more than life. But I won't see you this side of the river. Wait for me if you go first and we'll cross together. I'll do the same. Davey."

She never told Harley about the note. She had showed it to Missy who waited years to divorce him. She never gave up hope.

Chapter 8

Sarge knew he had nothing to do with Papa Smurf's discharge instructions, and since he had no next of kin, he truly hoped the old man would die in his sleep in the hospital.

Instead, he got better with each passing day. The drugs and regular meals agreed with him, and soon they were looking for a bed in one of the local homes. Sarge was assigned the task of telling Papa Smurf he was being discharged to Twin Oaks Nursing Home. The discharge planner at the hospital had tried, but he took a swing at her and now it was left to him.

He was sitting on the side of his bed dressed in his clothes from the street. Someone had laundered and patched them up a bit. He had six new pair of boxer shorts and some socks in a bag.

"Let's go, Sarge," he said as he got to his feet.

"Papa Smurf, we aren't going back to the street. Well, you aren't anyway. They found you a bed in a nice place not too far from here. I think you'll…"

He never got to finish his sentence. The old man had lunged for the door, knocking the bedside rolling tray aside. He ran down the hall and out the emergency exit, setting off the alarm. One of the male nurses went after him, but he was long gone before the nurse even got to the door.

Sarge looked for him and after three days gave up the search. He'd find him one way or another.

And he was right. On the fifth day after the escape Buzz came to his place on the street and told him Papa Smurf was dying and needed his help.

He followed Buzz to an alley about three blocks from the gentrified area. He found the old man wrapped in the blankets of other veterans who stood watch. Sarge knelt beside his friend and fellow street dweller and took his hand. "Leave us," he told the others and they slowly disbanded, calling Papa Smurf's name as they left. "Except you, Buzz. I may need your help when he passes."

Sarge had been here before. Twenty-nine times so far that year. He took Papa Smurf's hand and held it between both of his. "It's gonna be okay," he mumbled to try and comfort the old man. "I promise."

Papa Smurf looked up at Sarge and Buzz. "You know I got kids right? And a wife? I don't guess there's any sense in trying to say I'm sorry now."

Sarge patted the old man's hand. "Regret's aren't important now, Papa Smurf. Only thing you got to worry about right now is you. You need to be at peace."

Papa Smurf closed his eyes. His breathing was labored now, but his face was unlined with the worries he had carried all these years on the street.

"It's always like this," Sarge confided in Buzz. "They always regret leaving their family. But there are reasons only they understand."

Buzz nodded as he took the old man's free hand. They sat watch through the night with their comrade, waiting for him to cross the river.

Chapter 9

"Granny, do you ever think they'll find my dad," Bella asked from the back seat. Nonie turned toward her and reached out her hand. "I don't know, honey. It's been a long time."

"Yes, I know. I just wish I knew where he was. I want to let him see that he didn't hurt me that night in the river."

They were packing the fifty bags of lunches and cookies for the homeless people in Richmond into the cargo area of Missy's van. Nonie had stopped searching their faces, hoping against hope one would be Davey. She stopped asking five years ago. Now she just went to serve her fellow human beings who were down on their luck.

Nonie had made the trek every year since Davey left. After an hour's ride to the church in Richmond they would meet up with the other volunteers. It was only three days until Christmas, and somehow this year Nonie had a sense of peace. *I think it's because I finally gave up. Maybe it's the universe's way of telling me to be grateful for what I have.*

This year she was even grateful for Harley. His "piecrust promise" was so easily broken, but truth be told, the moment she held Davey in her arms, nothing else really mattered. He was her only child, and he changed her life the moment they laid him on her belly. Ten years later, mama and daddy had died three weeks apart, leaving her with only Harley and Davey. She had no siblings; it ran in her mother's side of the family. There had never been multiple births to any of the women as far as they knew.

The girls were in the back seat jabbering away, and Missy was driving. The radio was playing Christmas songs. When Bing Crosby's "I'll be Home for Christmas" came on the radio, she changed the station. She had listened to that song every year hoping it had magical powers and she'd see Davey walking up the front walk, his duffle bag slung over his shoulder.

It never happened. Now that song only made her bitter.

Missy pulled the van into the parking lot of Our Lady of Lourdes Catholic Church. Forty or fifty people were milling around, waiting for instructions from the parish priest. He popped out of the church a few minutes after they arrived, a short man with a full head of bright, red hair. Gabby went up to him and got their packet with instructions and a map to their assigned territory over by the VA center in Church Hill.

A line had formed against the side of the building that housed the center. Missy handed twelve bags each to Nonie, Gabby, and Bella. She picked up the remainder and they headed toward their destination.

Nonie recognized a couple of the men from last year. She began handing out bags to the twenty-five men that were leaning up against the wall. Missy had gone across the street with Gabby. She turned just as Gabby had gently shaken one of the two men sitting on the sidewalk who appeared to be sleeping. The one with the white beard woke with a start. "That's Papa Smurf—we thought we'd lost him but Buzz and the Sarge have been taking real good care of him."

"I remember Papa Smurf," Nonie began, "But I don't recognize the other one. Buzz, did you say?"

"Yeah. He and Papa Smurf have been out here a long time. Viet Nam vets, you know. A lot of us guys wouldn't be alive 'cept for those two. Weird, though. Buzz usually takes off soon as he sees you ladies comin'. He says he don't need no preaching and he don't need no cookies. He usually hightails it outta here."

"I see. Well, I don't like too much preaching, either," Nonie countered. She watched as Missy gently shook the man called Buzz. She spoke to him for a moment, then moved closer. She said a few words to him, and he jumped up and grabbed his duffle bag and ran down the sidewalk. Gabby went after him, and Missy ran across the street toward Nonie, her arms waving wildly. "Nonie! Nonie! It's him. It's Davey."

Gabby had caught up with her father and she was struggling with his duffle bag, trying to get him to stop. Bella and Missy had him by both arms when Nonie, gasping for air, caught up with them.

"I'm telling you nice ladies, I am not Davey—whoever that is. Just leave me be, now. I'm going to go on about my business and I thank you for the nice cookies and such."

Nonie came around in front of him. She put her hands on his shoulders, and looked at his eyes. "Davey," was all she said. Buzz dropped to his knees in front of her.

"Mama, please. Let me go. I'm happy where I am with the guys. I did try to come back after I left. I did, but I couldn't."

"But, daddy—I'm all right," Gabby said.

"Yes, Gabby I know. And you too Missy, and Bella. I know you're fine. And Mama, I knew you were okay too—long as I was outta your lives. But, you see, I'm not all right. I still have the dreams. It's not gonna change. Not now. Not never."

"I can't let you live on the street, Davey," Nonie cried. "I can't do it. You are my only child."

The man they called Sarge had joined them, together with a police officer. "What's going on here," they said in unison.

"This is my son, Davey. My only son. We've been looking for him for fifteen years. Please, Davey. Come home with me. It will be okay."

"Buzz, are these your kin?" Sarge asked.

"Yes." By now, Davey had composed himself and was getting to his feet.

"Do you folks need assistance?" the officer asked.

"No, no. We're fine," Nonie said.

"I'll leave you then. Have a nice Christmas."

Sarge had his arm around Buzz; he was talking to him quietly. "Ladies, he wants to stay here. I'm sorry you found him. It probably would be best for everyone if you assumed he was dead."

The four women had a stunned look on their faces, but they parted so Buzz and Sarge could walk back to the place where they left Papa Smurf.

Chapter 10

"How do you think we missed him all these years," Missy asked, breaking the silence in the van on the way home.

"I don't know. I had even tried that Sarge person. He carries around the names and dog tags he's taken from the veterans who have died. I used to check with him right regular, but he didn't have Davey's tag. He never heard of Davey."

"Probably because he came later, and he only knew him as Buzz," Gabby said.

"Look, we'll keep working on him. Maybe he'll change his mind. It's been a long time, and he has been living on the street, so I think he has to come to terms with it all," Missy said.

"You do know and understand him, Missy," Nonie replied.

When Nonie got home, she sent the girls off. "I need to tell him myself without too much distraction," she said as she kissed each one of them goodbye.

She went in through the front door. Harley was asleep in him chair. She let the front door slam and he jumped up out of his chair. "What in Sam Hill…"he yelled.

"It's only me, Harley. I have some news for you."

She fixed them both a cup of coffee, brought it in, and sat in the chair next to his recliner. "I have a story to tell you. We found Davey in Richmond."

He listened without a word. When she finished, he sat his cup down. "Let's go get him," he said.

"No. Let's give it a few days. After all, it was a huge shock for everyone."

"That's an understatement," Harley countered. "I think he needs to be here with us, though. This is just almost beyond belief."

"I know, Harley."

"Did he offer any explanations?"

"No, he just said it was best, that he'd tried to come home several times. I think the way people looked at him, treated him, had a lot to do with it. It's hard when you don't fit in the only place you've ever called home."

"Most of those old battleaxes are dead by now."

"Not all, and legends stay a long time after you're dead."

She stood and took the cups into the kitchen. "The girls and Missy are coming tomorrow night to open their gifts. They they'll be back Christmas day for dessert."

There was no answer from the den, so Nonie went about the work of fixing dinner. They ate in silence.

*****

The next day was Christmas Eve. Nonie had fixed all kinds of desserts, including those from the cookie exchange at church. Missy and the girls were coming at seven that evening, and she had to admit her house looked beautiful.

At seven, Missy came in without the girls. "Where are Gabby and Bella?" Nonie asked.

"They're coming. They had some last minute wrapping to do."

Nonie nodded. How many times had she been late to her parent's house for Christmas?

"I have something to give you," Nonie said. She handed Missy the green photo album. "It has all of Davey's pictures in it, and I thought they should have it."

"Including the ones…"

"Yes, including the ones in the paper where he saved that little child that was burning from the Napalm. The newspaper article is in there too. He saved so many children that day."

Missy shook her head. "Thank you, Nonie."

"I was wondering, Missy. How did your husband react to the news that Davy is still alive?"

"He's fine; very glad we have some closure. He knows I love him. You can have more than one soul mate in a lifetime. He certainly is my second chance."

Headlights announced the arrival of the girls. Harley went to the door. "Need help with packages or anything," he yelled out.

"Yes, come help us, Grandpa."

Harley went outside to give the girls a hand with the packages. Standing between the two of them was Davey.

"Well, I'll be a son-of-a…." Harley said as he grabbed his son in his arms.

"Dad, I'm so sorry I…" He couldn't continue.

"No, Davey. I am the one who is sorry. Your mama, she never gave up on you. I did and I was wrong. So, what happened to change your mind?"

Davey look at Bella and Gabby. "They did. They came back and told me they had forgiven me a long time ago. How do you manage to forgive someone who almost killed you? And Papa Smurf, he was dying and all he could talk about was missing his family. All those years. I didn't want to have that kind of passing."

Harley couldn't speak. Bella and Gabby were heading for the door. They went into the house ahead of Harley and Davey.

"Come on, son. Your Mama has waited long enough."

The song "I'll be Home for Christmas" was playing on the radio. Nonie's voice rose above it, "Turn than damn thing off. I don't want to hear that song."

"No, wait," Harley yelled from the yard. With that, he and his son walked through the door.

"Merry Christmas, Mom," Davy said, just as *I'll be Home for Christmas* finished on the radio.

If You Marry Me

Julie Leverenz

For Mary

Chapter 1

The card said, "With Dearest Love, T." Aster herself had put the card inside the tiny envelope and perched it on a clear plastic stick. Last month's card said the same, as did the card for the month before, and every month since Aster started at the shop five months ago. She had quizzed Margaret, the shop's owner, but Margaret just said it was a standing order, called in by what sounded like somebody's secretary and charged to a Visa card someplace up in New York.

A few minutes earlier, Aster had double-parked The Flower Basket's pink and green van outside Bay Haven senior home, pressed the button on the dashboard to set the flashers going, and pulled the afternoon's last delivery out of the back. The open-weave basket held mums in yellow, orange, and rust—every blossom perfect, appropriate for this crisp October day.

As much as Aster Bloom hated her name, she loved her job. She loved the way people came into the shop with their faces in a big question mark and left with just the right plant or flower or balloon for the occasion. She loved the way people's expressions morphed from wary to delighted when they answered their doorbell. Well, okay, her name had helped her get this job, but still. If Ricky's name had been any better she would've kept it after he went to jail and she divorced his sorry self, but Aster Esterbrook? Never mind.

This afternoon's deliveries had been mostly happy flowers— birthdays, anniversaries, and I Love You's—peppered with a couple of sympathies and apologies. Aster liked them all. Every arrangement gave her a tiny window into a relationship, and she liked to make up stories about the sender and receiver. She'd had to stop pretending the customers were her family, though. It made her too sad. Glancing at the delivery ticket on the basket of mums—Liliana Rachman, Apartment 304—Aster imagined a shriveled-up lady in an overstuffed chair whose face lit up once a month when she read, "With Dearest Love, T."

Holding the basket high, Aster marched up the broad, tiled steps and through the automatic glass doors, remembering Margaret's instructions to put on a show for any residents in the lobby. Sure enough, three elderly, hopeful faces turned and watched her approach the reception alcove. Beyond them, a wall of mullioned windows revealed an expansive lawn leading down to Hampton Roads harbor, where boats flying colorful spinnakers shone in the afternoon sun as they drifted past Fort Wool. Aster smiled at the residents. "Beautiful day," she said.

The cheerful young man behind the counter stood and reached for the basket. "Hi Aster," he said. "Gorgeous as always..."

Aster spoke the next line with him. "...and I don't mean the flowers." They laughed at the familiar ritual. "Hey, Corey. How's my favorite under-employed business major?"

"Same old, same old. Who're these for?"

"Liliana Rachman," Aster said, enjoying the way the name rolled off her tongue. "Apartment 304."

Corey's face fell. "Oh dear. I think she's in the hospital." He rummaged through some papers. "Yes, Peninsula General, Room 432. Can you take them over there?"

In spite of herself, Aster blurted, "What happened? Is she okay?" Over the five months she had been delivering the monthly flowers, Aster had invented stories about Liliana Rachman and felt that she knew her, in an imaginary sort of way. But Corey's face closed up ever so slightly, and Aster hastened to say, "No, no, I know you can't tell me. It's just that... never mind. Of course I'll take them. Thanks, have a great day."

Aster called Margaret to explain why she'd be late getting back from her deliveries and headed over to the hospital. On impulse, she strode past the hospital's information desk, where she usually left deliveries, straight to the elevators and up to the fourth floor. As she walked down the hallway, past carts of medical supplies and machines, she returned the beaming smiles and compliments of nurses and visitors, hiding her increasing trepidation. The corridor teemed with purpose and efficiency, but Aster sensed the stark emotions emanating from the patients' rooms. Desperation, hope, anxiety, resignation—everything she had felt in the terrifying days after her father's accident, up to the devastating moment of his death.

Aster's step faltered. *What am I doing here?* she thought. She reminded herself she was delivering a happy bouquet to a sick person. No harm in that. But really, she was just being nosy.

The door to room 432 was closed. Aster shifted from foot to foot, feeling awkward. The smell of antiseptic overpowered everything; Aster dipped her nose into the bouquet and could not find any fragrance. *This is a bad idea,* she thought. But just as she decided to go back and leave the flowers downstairs after all, a nurse bustled past and said cheerily, "Just knock and go on in. She keeps it closed because we're so noisy out here."

Aster took a deep breath and knocked lightly on the door. No response. *Maybe she's deaf,* she thought, and knocked harder. The wide door yielded under her knock. A surprisingly low, strong voice said, "Come in." Leading with the basket, Aster entered, then stopped, amazed.

The woman in the bed was breathtakingly beautiful, with a smooth, almost translucent face, framed by gorgeous waves of white hair. She could have been seventy or a hundred—to Aster, old people were, well, old—but she had never seen an old person with such flawless skin.

Aster began to speak, but the woman raised her hand, commanding silence, then looked intently at Aster for what seemed an eternity. Finally the woman ordered, "Put those on the windowsill and bring that chair over here." Aster balked at the woman's tone, so inconsistent with that beautiful face, but she set down the basket as commanded and slid the visitor chair over to the bed, careful not to disturb the IV tower and tubes snaking into the papery-thin back of the woman's hand.

"Sit down."

Aster sat.

"What's your name?"

"Aster, ma'am. Aster Bloom."

"No need to 'ma'am' me, Aster Bloom. It's charming, but I lived in New York for over sixty years and 'ma'am' makes me feel even older than I am. You may call me Lana."

Aster stifled a squeak of disappointment. How could anyone abide a nickname when they had a name as beautiful as Liliana?

"How old are you?"

"Twenty-four, ma' – Lana." *Habits sure can be hard to break,* Aster thought.

"Tell me about yourself."

Aster took a breath. She felt like she was in a job interview. "Well, I work for a flower shop and I'm going to night school at Thomas Nelson Community College."

"What are you studying?"

"Business and accounting. It's my first semester. It's pretty hard, but I was always good with numbers."

"Good for you," Lana said. "What will you do when you graduate?"

Aster looked sheepish. "I can't say, really. If I can afford it, I'd like to go on to Christopher Newport University. But I might just get a job around here somewhere." A hint of pride crept into her voice. "I was born and raised in Newport News."

"That's pitiful," Lana said.

"Excuse me?"

"A pretty girl like you should be traveling the world, seeing things, experiencing things. Then you can come back to Virginia when you're old. If you want to."

"Is that what you did?"

Lana ignored the question. "You're young, you should have bigger dreams."

Aster bristled at Lana's rudeness and presumption, but she thought, *She's an old lady. You have to make allowances.* She changed the subject. "I'm pleased to finally meet you, Lana. I've been delivering your flowers for five months. Somebody must love you a lot."

"Hmph," Lana said. "Who are your people? What does your father do?"

Good grief, she doesn't let up, Aster thought. *Are all New Yorkers this pushy?* She was tempted to snap, "My daddy's dead," and march out of the room. It was really none of Lana's business. But in spite of herself, Aster was intrigued. Clearly, Lana wouldn't talk about herself, and Aster wondered why. "My daddy's family is from Kentucky," she said. "He came here to work in the shipyard. I have some kin back there, but Daddy always said he came from a long line of jockeys and horse thieves." Aster gave an embarrassed laugh. *What possessed me to say that?*

"That explains your slender build," Lana said. "How about your mother?"

"Mama was a Ridgeway," Aster said. "She was an only child, like me. Mama died when I was two. Daddy and Gran raised me." She looked down at the floor. "They're both gone now. It's just me." *Ricky doesn't count,* she thought.

Lana's face softened. "You poor dear." She reached out her untethered hand and patted Aster's arm. "I'm so sorry. Every young child needs a mother."

Aster looked up in surprise. "That's what Gran used to say. She always made sure I knew my mother; showed me pictures and told me stories over and over till I could tell them myself." Aster tapped her chest. "Gran said my mother is here, in my heart." *And now she and Daddy are here, too.*

"Your grandmother was a very wise woman." Lana adjusted a pink satin bed jacket around her shoulders. "Tell me one of the stories about your mother."

Aster shifted in her chair; she hadn't talked about her mother in a long time. But she glimpsed a genuine interest in the old woman's eyes that belied her blunt words. Suddenly Aster yearned to share her mother's stories.

"Well, Mama—her name was Christine, but everybody called her Chrissy—loved animals. Gran said Chrissy would've rounded up all the stray dogs and cats in Warwick County, given the chance. She rescued a litter of six kittens that a farmer was getting ready to drown and stayed up nights, feeding them with an eyedropper. Gran drew the line, though, the day she hauled a possum out of the woods; just marched right into the house carrying it upside down by the tail."

Lana clapped her hands like a little girl. "I would have liked your mother."

"Mama started the county's first animal shelter when she was still in high school. We always had cats and dogs from there when I was little. There's even a little sign in the shelter's foyer with her name on it."

"I look forward to hearing more of your stories, Aster. Are you married? Children?"

Aster shrugged. "Was married. Not any more. No kids." She tried again. "How about you?"

Lana's gaze drifted, focusing on something only she could see. "I never married," she said quietly. Her eyes snapped back with a guarded look, as if she'd been caught revealing a secret. "Electrolytes." Lana raised the hand with the tubes in it. "They tell you to drink lots of water but they don't tell you how much is too much. Evidently there is a balance."

Aster struggled to keep up with the conversation's direction. "I beg your pardon?"

"I drank too much water and an imbalance made me lose my balance." Lana twinkled and Aster laughed. "At least I didn't break anything when I fainted. They tell me they're keeping me for observation."

As if on cue, a nurse came in with a blood pressure cart.

"This is Bonnie, the best nurse on the planet," Lana said. "Bonnie, this is my friend Aster."

"Oh, Miz Rachman, how you go on." Bonnie turned to Aster with a big smile. "Isn't she the sweetest thing? We all just love her to pieces."

Aster nodded, startled to be dubbed Lana's friend and not at all sure about the "sweetest thing" bit. She stood up to make room for Bonnie. "Well, I'd best be going. It was very nice to meet you, Lana."

"Come back and visit me, darling girl. Any time. I want to hear more stories. And you must tell me about those accounting classes."

"I will," Aster said, kicking herself as soon as she said it.

Chapter 2

Lana's prying questions and bossiness annoyed Aster. But a spark of curiosity lingered in the back of her mind—who was "T"? And why was Lana so secretive about her past? Gran had never tired of talking about herself and what she knew about her family.

The next day, Aster saved the two arrangements for Peninsula General for last. She told herself she would drop in on Lana for just a minute, and that would be the end of it. When she got to Room 432, she found Lana sitting like a queen in the big chair, wearing a light blue sweater with tiny pearl buttons, navy blue slacks, and low-heeled navy pumps on her primly crossed feet. A delicate silver locket hung around her neck, with matching earrings dangling from her ears. Her hair and makeup looked expertly done.

Lana clapped her hands. "There you are, darling girl." She pressed her hands to the arms of the chair and pushed herself up. When she wobbled, Aster rushed to steady her. "Thank you, dear. Give me a hug," Lana said, wrapping her arms around Aster's neck and giving a fierce squeeze. Aster squeezed back, but gently, feeling the old woman's fragile bones beneath the sweater.

"Oooh," Aster said, stroking the sweater. "This is so soft."

"Cashmere," Lana said dismissively, easing herself back into the chair.

A hospital employee came in and introduced herself as the social worker. "I am here with your discharge instructions, Mrs. Rachman," she said in a loud, schoolmarmish voice.

"I am *Miss* Rachman," Lana said, equally loudly. "Not Mrs. And I am not deaf."

"Oh. Sorry." The woman turned to Aster. "Medical transport is downstairs. An orderly will be here in a minute with a wheelchair. Will you—"

Lana interrupted. "Aster will meet us at Bay Haven. Won't you, dear?"

Trapped, Aster stuttered, "Uh, okay. I guess I can do that."

Which was how, an hour later, Aster found herself standing in Lana's apartment, watching Lana submit, barely, to the solicitous ministrations of an aide. "This is Janine," Lana had said when Janine met them at the elevator, "the best little aide on the planet." Aster and Janine both laughed.

While Lana and Janine fussed at each other, Aster took the opportunity to survey Lana's compact living space. A kitchenette with sink, microwave, and refrigerator—no stove—was tucked along one side of the entry hall, with the handicap-accessible bathroom across from it. The main room held a brocade sofa in shades of deep burgundy and green, flanked by end tables in dark wood and a pair of fancy lamps. The lamps looked like they were made from the same green and white material as the cameo that had belonged to Aster's mother—Wedgwood, somebody said. Through another door was a small bedroom, its single bed topped by a burgundy and green satin spread, and a dark wood dresser with a huge, gold-rimmed mirror. Aster had never been in a rich person's home before.

Aster walked over to the sitting room window and looked down at the harbor, where a stately container ship, piled high with colorful, railcar-sized boxes of goods from overseas, plowed through the channel. An oyster boat scurried out of its lumbering path. Aster lingered, thinking she could stand here forever.

A few minutes later, Janine departed with a final, "Pull the bell if you need anything, Miss Rachman." Lana took her walker and said, "Come, Aster, we will go through the mail." Aster gave the container ship a tiny farewell wave, then turned and helped Lana make her way to the ornately carved desk. It was littered with envelopes and junk mail.

*****

That night, Aster sat at her best friend's kitchen table, forking meatballs into her mouth in between attempts to mimic Lana's regal voice. "You will now help me with my mail," Aster announced with a fake New York accent. Winnie hooted.

"I couldn't believe it," Aster continued. "Ninety percent of her mail was junk, and you know why? Because she gives money to everything. Not a lot—ten dollars here, twenty there—but she has no clue about computers or mail merge. She thinks she's obligated to respond if she gets a personalized letter."

"She's a prime mark," said Ben. Ben was Winnie's husband and one of the top insurance agents on the Peninsula. "Charities and scams love old people."

"Yeah, I can't help but worry about that."

"So what are you going to do?" Winnie asked.

"Well, she's kind of interesting, in a bossy sort of way. I told her I'd come by again on Saturday. Besides, I'm still curious about this 'T' person."

"Is she insured?" Ben asked. Winnie jabbed his bicep. "Ow!" He wagged a finger at her. "Insurance keeps you in meatballs, sweetheart." Winnie rolled her eyes.

"I dunno," Aster said, laughing.

Winnie passed the salad to Aster. "Changing the subject," she said, "I found you the perfect guy today."

"Quit, Winnie," Aster said with a sigh. Winnie had been pushing "perfect" men at her since the day she filed for divorce. "Stop trying to fix me up. I've told you, I'm done with men."

After her father's death and her disastrous marriage, Aster had convinced herself that friends were all she needed. The love that she carried around in her memories of her father and Gran was more than enough. "Besides," she continued, "just because you were right about Ricky only means you know who's not perfect. Perfect is impossible."

"I found Ben, didn't I?"

"Yeah, but you kept him to yourself, you selfish thing, you," said Aster. Ben tilted back in his chair, grinning.

"No, really, this guy is absolutely perfect," Winnie said. "We're helping him find a condo. He's a dentist." Winnie was a secretary in a realtor's office, studying for her real estate license.

Ben brought his chair upright with a crash. "By definition, a dentist can't be perfect," he sputtered.

Winnie jerked her head at her husband and said to Aster, "Ben's a dentist-phobe from way back. Trust me on this, Aster. He's tall, blond, blue eyes, nice voice, polite…"

"So why's he not married?"

"Why don't you ask him? Can I give him your number?"

"No!" Aster almost shouted. "I'm… I'm not ready to start dating again. I've only been divorced a—"

"—year and a half," Winnie said. "That's plenty long enough. Sure, Ricky was a con man. He stole from you, he lied to you, he was bad news all around." Aster winced. Winnie patted her shoulder and said, "Most guys aren't like Ricky. It's time you got back out there, girlfriend. This guy's name is Andrew Collins. Think about it, before somebody else snaps him up."

On Saturday, as Aster approached the reception counter at Bay Haven, Corey came out from the back office and gave her a big smile. "Wow, since when are you making Saturday deliveries?"

"I'm just a visitor today, Corey."

Corey read upside down as Aster signed in to visit Lana. "She's got her hooks into you too, huh? We all hop to when she says, 'Jump.'"

"She's an amazing lady," Aster said.

"Yep, you got that right." Corey leaned on the counter. "Say, is there any chance I could buy you a coffee later on? I'm off at three."

Aster considered it, remembering Winnie's urgings. Corey seemed harmless enough; it might be a way to see if she really was ready to "get back out there." Noting the mixture of fear and hope in Corey's face, she took pity on him. "Sure, why not," she said, but her smile was uncertain.

Upstairs on the third floor, the door to Lana's apartment was unlatched. When Aster rang the bell, Lana called, "Come right in, dear. It's open." Aster found Lana seated at the desk, with the mail neatly stacked before her. The chair that Aster had moved next to the desk last week was already in position. "You're right on time," Lana said, sounding like a supervisor with a time clock. Aster made a mental note never to be late.

After her visit with Lana, Aster met Corey at Starbucks. She knew that Corey was taking graduate business classes, but she was surprised to learn that his undergraduate accounting classes at Christopher Newport University had been almost identical to the ones she was taking at the community college, right down to using the same textbook.

"That makes me feel better," she said. "I always thought university classes were different. More advanced."

Corey made a face. "It looks like accounting is accounting, wherever you take it. And I'm starting to wonder why I spent all that money at CNU when I could have taken the same classes at TNCC for a lot less."

"I would love to be at CNU," Aster said wistfully. "I hope to finish there. Assuming I make it through this class." She sighed. "I've always been good with numbers, but accounting is way more than just numbers. And my professor doesn't explain things very well."

"I'm the opposite," Corey confessed. "Accounting makes sense to me. It's the math I don't get."

Aster arched her eyebrows and grinned. "Well," she said, in a saucy, Bogart voice, "Louis, I think this is the beginning—"

"—of a beautiful friendship," Corey finished, grinning back.

*****

Aster's Saturdays turned into a weekly routine: two o'clock with Lana, followed by coffee with Corey. Each week as they went through the mail, Aster learned a tiny bit more about Lana. Settling a question about a bill required giving Lana's birth date; she would be ninety-three years old next May. After Aster explained the concept of automatic mailings, Lana agreed to be more selective with her contributions, but she insisted on giving to her alma mater and the hospice center that had cared for a dear friend. Pension payments came from Verizon, which had absorbed Lana's former employer, New York Telephone.

"I was the only woman in the accounting department," Lana said proudly. "Except for the secretaries, of course."

"You were an accountant!" Aster said with delight. "Wasn't that hard, back then?"

"Oh, the men didn't know what to make of me at first." Lana shrugged. "Some of them said unpleasant things. But one day a Vice President came down to where we were all working. He came over to my desk and said, 'Miss Rachman, if you ever need anything, you come straight to me.'" She laughed. "I never had any problems after that."

Aster began to understand where Lana's abrupt manner came from: having to deal with being the only woman in a man's profession for all those years.

Eventually, Aster learned that Lana had indeed spent her early years on the Peninsula, moved to New York as a teenager, then came back to Virginia last year. When Aster asked why she didn't stay in New York, Lana simply said, "All of my friends are dead. And I never liked the cold." But despite Aster's gentle questions, Lana never mentioned her family, or what took her to New York so many years ago. She always changed the subject, often asking for another story about Lana's mother. Aster began to wonder if Lana's independence had been thrust on her, instead of being a choice. Either way, Aster dreamed that she, too, could be independent and successful.

As for her other Saturday companion, Corey turned out to be a nice enough guy, if a little dull. He wasn't much to look at: dumpy, with thinning hair and a sallow complexion. Nothing a gym membership couldn't fix, Aster thought—except the hair. Corey lived at home with his mother and two younger sisters while pursuing a part-time Masters in Business at Old Dominion University. His mother was a bank teller, and Corey's plan was to be a bank manager.

Aster found herself parroting Lana's admonitions to dream bigger. "Wouldn't you like to travel, see places?" she asked Corey one afternoon.

"Lord, yes," he said. "I'd love to see California. Big Sur, the Golden Gate Bridge. How about you?"

"Holland—the Netherlands," Aster said. "I'd love to see the tulips. And the flower auction."

The next Saturday, Aster brought an advertisement she found for the Monterey Peninsula. To her delight, Corey handed her a brochure for Amsterdam. Aster began to think Corey might not be so dull, after all.

Chapter 3

On a chilly mid-November morning, Aster helped a mink-clad, white-gloved, and mesh-scarfed Lana into the front seat of Aster's tired old Honda CR-V. The white gloves and scarf explained Lana's incredible complexion and alabaster hands, amazing for a woman who would soon be ninety-three years old. Aster looked at the backs of her own hands, remembering all the freckles and sunburns.

If I'd known, I would have gotten this heap washed and vacuumed, Aster thought as she lifted Lana's right foot over the sill and fastened her seat belt for her. But Lana had telephoned The Flower Basket first thing that morning, and when Aster arrived, Margaret handed Aster a tidy Thanksgiving-themed arrangement and said, "Don't take off your coat. Miss Rachman wants to borrow you this morning."

"What exactly does that mean?" said Aster.

"She decided that as long as you were going to deliver her flowers today anyway, perhaps I would permit you to take her to an appointment. She offered to pay me for your time."

Aster wasn't sure if she should be flattered or offended. "What did you tell her?"

"I said it was a slow day, and we would be happy to provide this service to such a good customer. So go on. Her appointment is at eleven."

*****

At the professional building, Aster unfolded Lana's walker and helped her inside.

"Liliana Rachman for my appointment with Dr. Harrison," Lana announced. Aster admired the cadence of Lana's voice as she spoke her full, melodious name.

"Miss Rachman, how lovely to see you again," the receptionist trilled. "The hygienist is ready for you."

Aster settled herself in the waiting room. She was engrossed in an old copy of People magazine, wondering how on earth people like Brad and Angelina could even pretend to have normal lives, when the receptionist approached her. "Could you come through? There seems to be a bit of a problem."

The receptionist led Aster back into the maze of offices. Aster heard Lana's voice echo down the hall, shouting, "I must see Dr. Harrison." In the treatment room, she found Lana in the dental chair, flanked by a frightened-looking hygienist and a tall young man in a white coat, presumably the dentist.

The dentist said in a calm, soothing voice, "I understand, Miss Rachman, but Dr. Harrison was called to the hospital for an emergency procedure." Aster noted with approval his use of "Miss". He continued, "I am Dr. Collins. I graduated from dental school first in my class, and I assure you, Dr. Harrison would not have asked me to join his practice if he didn't think I would take very good care of our patients."

He turned to Aster and held out his hand. "Andrew Collins," he said.

Aster blinked. *The perfect Andrew Collins.* "Aster Bloom," she said. When their hands clasped, a tremor shot up her arm and momentarily stopped her heart. *This isn't happening,* she thought. *I'm done with men.* She managed a weak smile as they both turned their attention to Lana.

Dr. Collins was unflappably courteous in the face of Lana's suspicions and questions, even when she demanded to see his diploma. He sent reassuring glances Aster's way as if to say, "Don't worry, I've got this."

Lana put on her glasses and scrutinized the diploma. "Why didn't you say right away that you went to NYU?" she said, handing it back to him. "You may proceed."

At the end of the appointment, Lana declared Andrew the best dentist on the planet. "Aster and I are going to lunch at Bon Appetit," she declared. "You must join us, Dr. Collins."

Aster blanched. "I'm sure Dr. Collins has other patients, Lana."

Andrew Collins smiled, and Aster struggled not to blush under his quietly appraising gaze. "As a matter of fact," he said, "my next patient is at two. I would be honored to join you, ladies."

That evening, Aster held the phone away from her ear as Winnie shrieked, "I told you! I can't wait to tell Ben. I knew it. We'll have to invite him for Thanksgiving."

"Wait, wait," Aster cried. "Hold on now. He had lunch with Lana. You'd have thought he was her long-lost nephew or something, the way she fussed over him. I was just there."

"Yeah, yeah, don't kid yourself. So we'll invite Her Majesty too. Oh, this'll be perfect."

Aster disconnected, marveling at the way Winnie made things sound perfect, even if they weren't. Aster felt torn between elation and terror. She'd never had the best sense about men, and she had come to prize her independence. Ricky had seemed perfect at first, too—charming, handsome, clever, sexy—and Aster had no reason to trust the tingle she felt when Andrew took her hand.

*****

Thanksgiving Dinner was a lively meal at Winnie and Ben's. Both Lana and Andrew agreed to come, and Winnie and Ben, with Aster's help, cooked a huge turkey and their favorite side dishes. Lana ordered a spectacular, low centerpiece from The Flower Basket and Andrew brought four bottles of the most excellent sauvignons any of them had tasted. Andrew traded New York stories with Lana, who basked under the attention, and was comfortable talking real estate with Winnie and insurance with Ben. Sitting next to Andrew, Aster felt surprisingly shy, unable to summon any of her usual easy banter. She didn't have much experience with boisterous gatherings like this; Thanksgivings with her father and Gran had been bountiful, but subdued. *Gran would have loved being here*, Aster thought, remembering how hard Gran had worked to make Thanksgiving and

Christmas the family's happiest, most loving celebrations. *Her stories would have this group in stitches.* Aster felt a sharp pang of loss.

Pulling her attention back to the table, Aster did her part by prompting Ben to tell his best jokes and was fascinated to hear about Lana's and Andrew's travels. The conversation swirled around her. Staying in the background suited her fine, and she was first to jump up to get more food or clear the table.

After dinner, Aster helped Winnie put up the leftovers and load the dishwasher. She was scrubbing pots, halfway up to her elbows in a sinkful of hot, soapy water, when Andrew came in.

"Need any help?" he said.

"Brilliant timing," Winnie said. "We're just about finished. How do men do that?"

"It's a gift," he said, taking the dishtowel from Winnie's hands. "Give me that. Now I can claim that I helped." Winnie took off her apron, winked at Aster, and left them alone.

Andrew took a pot out of the dish rack and began to dry it. Beside him, Aster's tongue froze in her mouth. "Are you always this quiet?" he said.

Aster dredged her voice up from its hiding place. "I'm not much for talking when I don't have anything to say," she said, feeling like an idiot and sure she sounded like one.

"I wish more people were like that," he said. "Maybe that's why I became a dentist. My patients can't talk." Aster giggled. "Ah, that's better," he said. He handed the pot to Aster and she put it on the shelf. "I like your friends," he said. "And Lana is really something, isn't she." He made it a statement, not a question, so Aster just nodded. She searched desperately for a way to keep the conversation going.

"So," she said, "what are your plans for Christmas?"

Andrew dried his hands and hung the dishtowel on the stove handle. "I'll be in New York with my parents and sister, then I've got an engagement party on the twenty-sixth."

"That sounds like fun," Aster said. "Friends of yours?"

Andrew laughed. "No, silly—me. Didn't I tell you? I'm getting married next summer."

Suddenly Winnie appeared in the doorway behind Andrew. Her eyes told Aster she had heard. "Oops," she mouthed. Winnie took Andrew's arm and beckoned to Aster. "Lana's getting tired, I think it's time to call it a day."

Aster squared her shoulders, pasted a smile on her face, and resolved never, ever, to let Winnie get her hopes up again.

The following Monday evening, a class night, Aster left work promptly at six thirty. Crossing the street to her car, she saw a man leaning against a light post, watching her. Aster paused. She looked up and down the street, glad to see there were other people around, enjoying the unseasonably warm November evening.

The man sauntered over to her. "Hey, cutie." He wore the nonchalant expression she had loved, then despised.

"Ricky." She took a step back. "How'd you get out?"

"Good behavior. You know me."

Yeah, I know you. "What do you want?"

"Just wanted to see you again. Absence makes the heart fonder and all." He unleashed his most charming smile. To Aster, it looked more like a menacing leer. "I see you're just as cute as ever. Letting your hair grow." He reached out and touched a strand of brown hair that curled over her shoulder.

Aster brushed his hand away. "Cut it, Ricky. What do you want?"

"Looks like you're moving in fine company now, Aster. Old ladies in mink, doctors—you're comin' up in the world. I figure you probably have some extra you could spare for Ricky, for old times' sake."

Aster was appalled. "Are you spying on me?" Ricky shrugged.

"In case you've forgotten," she said, "you conned me out of 'most all of the money my daddy left me. We are divorced. I have nothing for you, not now, not ever." She reached for the door handle of her car. "Go away. I've got a class to get to."

Ricky gripped her arm. "You owe me, cutie," he growled.

"In your dreams, Ricky. Let go or I'll scream." A couple walking toward them hesitated. Flashing a benign smile, Ricky released her. The couple hurried by.

Ricky hissed, "You owe me because I left you out of it. We had some kicks, didn't we, cutie, me grabbing the goods and you scratching off in the getaway car. Who took that license plate off, huh?"

"One time, Ricky. One time." Aster opened the car door.

"A lot more than one time driving the getaway car, wasn't it, cutie. We were a team." Ricky's cocky expression faltered. "I thought you loved me; that's why I protected you."

Aster shook her head and climbed into her car, struggling to contain her panic.

Before she could close the door, Ricky leaned in and whispered, "I'll bet your mink lady and that doctor would love to hear all about it."

Aster shrank away. "You wouldn't."

"Watch me," he said. "Hey, I know you, Aster. You have to process this. That's fine. You just give it some thought. How about we think of it as my Christmas present." He grabbed her hand and kissed it before she could jerk it back. "Ta ta, cutie. I'll call you."

Aster slammed the door and sat, trembling, while Ricky strolled down the sidewalk. At the corner, he gave a jaunty wave, then he was gone. Her hands gripped the steering wheel, then she put her head down and sobbed.

Chapter 4

Aster stumbled through the rest of the week in a daze. She went to work and class feeling like a robot on autopilot. At night, her brain spun in circles, keeping her awake, sorting through options, none of which had happy endings. She begged off Saturday with Lana and Corey, giving the lame excuse of having to study for exams. She kept her phone chats with Winnie superficial and breezy. She couldn't face any of them. Ricky was spying on her; she didn't dare risk a confrontation in front of her friends. What could she say? "Sorry, folks, but I helped my ex-husband steal stuff?" No, this was her problem. She would handle it. Somehow.

At least she still had the flowers. For a few hours each day, she lost herself in their beauty and focused only on creating exquisite arrangements. Next to the happy faces of the recipients, Aster loved the moment just before she closed the doors to the van, when she looked inside and saw the rows of flowers and plants neatly arranged, each one made especially to express the sender's feelings—joy, sorrow, love. She wished it could be that easy for her to express herself. Wouldn't it be nice if she could be an orchid for Lana, a bunch of daisies for Corey, a fistful of straw for Winnie—in honor of Andrew—and a cactus for Ricky?

Waiting for Ricky's call was torture. She had no plan; she didn't know what she would say, and the threat of his unknown demands gnawed at her. Days went by with no call, then a week. She called his mother, but Mrs. Esterbrook didn't even know he was out of jail. Aster buried herself in flowers and in her books, beginning to hope that he would leave her alone, that his threats were just empty posturing. But everywhere she went she looked over her shoulder and worried.

On the evening of her accounting exam, Aster left the classroom feeling confident that she had done well. Around her, the other students compared notes on some of the more difficult questions and congratulated each other on surviving another semester. Aster envied their high spirits. Keeping close to the group, she searched for a lone figure lurking under street lights, on the sidewalk, among the cars. She wondered how long she would have to live with this dread.

Later, Aster's phone rang as she unlocked the door and entered her apartment. She dropped her purse on the sofa, pulled the phone from her pocket, and with trembling hands, checked the ID. Her racing heart calmed immediately. "Hi Winnie," she said. "Exams are over, thank God. I think I did okay."

"I'm sure you did better than okay, what with all the studying you claim you had to do," Winnie said. Aster pretended not to hear the sarcasm in her friend's voice. "Tell you what, why don't we have lunch tomorrow."

"You, me, and what 'perfect' guy this time, Winnie?"

"I'm shocked at your flagrant lack of faith in me," Winnie said, with exaggerated hurt. "How could I know Andrew was engaged? From now on, I promise I will interrogate every man with fifteen pages of questions before I let him anywhere near you."

Aster laughed. "You sound like my Daddy," she said, thinking, *Daddy all but did that with Ricky, but did I pay him any mind?* "Anyway, I can't do tomorrow. Margaret needs me all day."

"Friday, then," Winnie said. "We'll go to The Lunch Bell and drown your sorrows in Betty's chocolate pie."

The next day, Aster arrived early at The Flower Basket and checked her day's orders. Seeing Lana's December delivery at the top of the list, Aster's mood lifted—this was her chance to make amends with Lana, and Corey too, if he was working. She went into the walk-in cooler and surveyed the flowers. *Red and white carnations for Lana this month*, she thought. *Nestled in holly.*

Driving over to Bay Haven late that afternoon, Aster rehearsed her apologies. In the lobby, the reception desk was empty. Aster felt a stab of disappointment. She hadn't realized how much she was looking forward to seeing Corey. Just as she finished signing the visitor book, Corey stepped out of the back office.

"Corey!" she said, "I'm so glad you're here."

His voice was noncommittal. "Hey, Aster."

"Listen," she said, stumbling over her words, "I'm sorry about last week. I guess you had exams too? How did they go?"

He crossed his arms. "Okay."

She regarded him, then set Lana's flowers on the counter and crossed her arms too. "Okay," she said. "How many cookies will I have to buy you later to clear that pout off your face?"

Corey face remained set, but Aster detected a tiny crinkle around his eyes.

"At least two," he said.

On the third floor, Lana's apartment door was closed. Aster rang the bell and after a moment, Janine opened the door. "Oh hello, Miss Aster," Janine said in her lovely Jamaican lilt. "Miss Rachman's resting. She had a bit of a turn this morning. Come on in."

As she made her way through the sitting room, Aster noticed the jumbled mail piled on the desk.

In the bedroom, Lana lay under a fleece throw, looking small and frail. She raised a limp hand. "Hello, darling girl," she said. A wave of confusion crossed her face. "Is it Saturday?"

"No, Lana, it's Thursday. I brought your December flower arrangement." Aster held it up where Lana could see. "Carnations and holly. For Christmas. I made it myself."

"They're lovely, dear." Lana gave Aster a weak smile. "I am so glad to see you. I didn't know if you would come again."

Aster felt terrible. "Oh, Lana, I'm so sorry about last week." She set the flowers on the dresser and crouched by the bed, repeating, "I'm so sorry."

Lana patted Aster's cheek. "Well you're here now; that's what's important. We have a lot of mail to go through." Lana's voice sharpened. "Unless you have somewhere else to be?"

"I can stay, Lana," Aster said meekly. "Shall I bring the mail in here?"

Lana raised herself on her elbows. "No, I will get up." Aster shot an alarmed glance at Janine, who leaned against the door jamb, looking amused. Aster felt like shouting at Janine, "How can you laugh at this little old lady? She's so helpless and weak." But she knew she was really berating herself for abandoning Lana last Saturday.

Under Janine's watchful eye, Aster helped Lana stand up and use her walker to go to the desk. Noting how Lana was out of breath, Aster said, "Are you sure you're up to this?"

"If I get tired, I'll rest," Lana said firmly. "We have work to do." She gave Janine a dismissive wave. "Thank you, Janine dear."

It took extra time to go through all the mail, and Aster called down to Corey to say she would be late for their coffee.

"Tell you what," Corey said. "How about we meet for pizza later?"

"Sure," Aster said. "If I remember, Angelo's even has cookies."

Corey laughed. "Works for me. See ya."

Lana gave Aster a knowing smile. "You and our young Corey, hm?" she said.

"We're just friends," Aster said. "Don't you go getting ideas, Lana."

"I thought you had your cap set for Dr. Andrew Collins?"

"I don't have my 'cap set' for anyone, Lana," Aster protested. "I'm going to be an independent woman with lots of friends. Besides," she added, feeling mischievous, "why should I tell you about the men in my life when you've never told me about yours?"

Watching Lana's face close into an impenetrable mask, Aster feared she had gone too far. But after a moment, Lana's expression cleared and she gave a light, tinkling laugh. "You have a valid point, my dear. Let me see. I do recall a certain young man who was quite sweet on me. Dashing fellow, a friend of a friend. He had an airplane, flitted around the country on some kind of very important business. He took me flying once. Such fun!"

Aster leaned forward, eager to hear. "What happened?" she prompted.

"And then there was the European count. Oh my, he certainly knew how to treat a girl." Lana's eyes sparkled. "I remember one evening we were out for dinner in Manhattan with three other couples. They were all married, and all of the wives had their mink coats. He said to me, "Liliana, if you marry me, you will have a mink coat too.""

"Wow," Aster said, entranced.

"So the next day, I went downtown and bought myself a mink coat." Lana rested her hands in her lap. "And that was that."

Aster burst out laughing. "Oh, Lana, no man could possibly keep up with you, could they?"

"Um," said Lana, her gaze far away.

When Aster left Lana's apartment she spotted Janine coming out of another resident's room down the hall. "Janine! Do you have a minute?" Aster trotted over to the aide. "I was so worried when I saw Lana this afternoon, she looked so frail. Is she okay?"

Janine laughed. "Oh, don't you worry about Miss Rachman. She has her spells, but she's tough, that one."

Later, at Angelo's, when Aster related her concerns to Corey, he laughed, too. "Haven't you figured her out yet?" he said. "Miss Liliana Rachman is a master manipulator. If she's called down to the desk once demanding attention, she's called a hundred times. She had our new director running up to her apartment three-four times a week until he figured it out." He lowered his voice in a not-bad imitation of Lana, "'Corey, darling boy, would you ask Mr. Thomas to come up right away? I must show him something.' She's not above having a sudden asthma attack if she doesn't get her way, either."

"Well, that makes me feel a little better. She looked like she had one foot in eternity, then she popped up like nothing was wrong."

"Welcome to our world." Corey took another piece of pepperoni and mushroom. "I hear the nurses and aides talking sometimes, and the littlest thing can throw these old people for a loop, or perk them right up. You're probably the best thing that's ever happened to Miss Rachman."

"I doubt that, but it's nice of you to say. She's helped me a lot with my class work, too. Almost as much as you have."

"At your service, Madame. Anything for that last piece of pizza."

*****

A chill wind blew across the parking lot when Aster walked to her car. Corey had gone back to Bay Haven to finish up next week's activities schedule. She tugged her watch cap farther over her ears.

"Miss me?" The taunting voice sounded right behind her. Aster froze, then instinctively lashed out. "God, Ricky, giving me a heart attack won't get you anything."

Ricky leaned in and Aster got a whiff of his aftershave: Axe. She recoiled. "Here's the deal," he growled. "I want a thousand dollars."

"A thousand dollars?" Aster sputtered, "You're crazy. I barely make enough to pay the rent."

"Oh, but your mink lady and your doctor man, I'm sure they're good for it." Ricky leaned closer, his acrid breath smelling of cigarettes. "Of course," he said, "there's always the other possibility. We were good together, Aster. We could be again."

Horrified, Aster took a step back. "Forget it, Ricky. No way, no how, never."

"Suit yourself. Call me when you have the money. Or if you change your mind about us." He slipped a piece of paper into her bag. "Here's my number. Call anytime, as long as it's soon."

A car drove by, slowed, and pulled into the parking lot. Corey got out. Aster raised her hand, warning him off. *Please, go away, Corey. You don't want any part of this.*

Corey came up beside them. "Karin did the activities schedule for me," he said pleasantly to Aster. He held out his hand to Ricky. "Corey Norcross."

"Corey Norcross." Ricky simpered. "Who's your pansy boy, Aster?"

Before Aster could spit out a retort, Corey put a staying hand on her arm. "There's no need to be rude, sir," Corey said. "Perhaps you should leave."

"Ooh, perhaps you should leave," Ricky parroted. "What're you gonna do, call your momma?" He jabbed a finger at Corey, who grabbed it, planted his feet, and neatly flipped Ricky onto the pavement.

Aster gaped at Corey, dumbstruck. Ricky scrambled to his feet, snarled, "I'm not done with you. Either of you," and limped away, rubbing his arm.

"Aster, are you okay? Who was that?" Corey asked.

In the distance, Ricky yelled, "Soon, Aster."

Corey took Aster's shoulders gently in his hands. She had never noticed how strong they were. "Talk to me," he said.

Aster debated how much to tell him. Finally she said, "That was my ex, Ricky. He's a total jerk, and he's trying to make me miserable." She straightened. "I'm not going to let him." Looking at Corey with frank admiration, she said, "But you, who knew you were a superhero?"

Chapter 5

The next morning, Aster woke in a sweat, having dreamed that she was in a courtroom, but this time she was the accused and Ricky was on the witness stand. She crawled out of bed, exhausted. In the bathroom mirror, she looked at her pale, blotchy skin and the dark circles under her red-rimmed eyes. *What am I going to do?* she thought. She couldn't bank on Corey showing up every time, even though she sensed that he would be happy to serve as her protector. She didn't want or need a protector. She had to learn how to take care of herself. And she wondered how happy Corey would really be if he knew the whole story.

She brushed her teeth and swirled Listerine in her mouth until her eyes watered. The mirror told her she looked exactly as miserable as she felt. She could soldier through work, but this was the day of her lunch with Winnie, and Winnie would know immediately that something was wrong. Seriously wrong. She contemplated canceling, but that would require explanation, too. With a long, tired sigh, Aster splashed cold water on her face and went to get dressed.

At twelve twenty-five Aster hurried to finish the altar arrangement for a church, knowing she would be late to meet Winnie. She slid in the last stalk of alstroemeria, set the arrangement on the deliveries table, and waved a hasty goodbye to Margaret.

At the real estate office, Winnie was beside herself. She jumped up and hustled Aster to the chair next to her desk. "Where've you been? You're too late."

"Too late? The Lunch Bell is still open." Aster had walked past it on her way from the parking garage.

Winnie looked disgusted. "Not that. He's already gone in for the closing."

Aster slumped in the chair and threw her head back. "You are hopeless. I don't know why I even talk to you."

"Because you love me. Now we'll have to wait till he comes out. He's gorgeous, Aster. Just moved here from Long Island—"

"Whoopee, another New Yorker."

Winnie ignored her. "—and he works at Jefferson Lab." She clasped her hands to her breast. "Imagine, a world famous scientist, a future Nobel Prize winner. He is beyond perfect."

At the word "perfect," Aster stood up. "I'm going for chocolate pie. You with me?"

"Oh, take off your coat, Aster. What can it hurt? You need to at least see him, he is soooo dreamy."

The outer door opened and a man stepped in. He was tall and slim, with olive skin and dark eyes, and wore a black overcoat, gloves, and a fedora.

"On the other hand…" Winnie said, jumping to her feet. "May I help you?"

"I hope I am not too late," the man said, with an accent Aster couldn't place. "I am Adnan Khouri. I was supposed to meet Michael Kingston here for the closing, but my plane was delayed."

"Of course," Winnie said. "I'll let him know you're here." Winnie hurried down the hall. When Aster smiled at the man, he averted his eyes.

A moment later, Aster could only agree that the man who loped down the hall before Winnie was, in fact, gorgeous. *Fabio with a good haircut,* she thought.

"Adnan! You made it!" the man exclaimed. They embraced—too long—then held each other at arms' length, beaming.

Winnie came and stood beside Aster. "Oops," she said.

That night, Aster slept soundly, dreaming of Arab princes in flowing robes. If nothing else, Winnie's misguided scheme had distracted her from worrying exclusively about Ricky. Even better, Aster had laughed herself into such a state that Winnie hadn't noticed the circles under her eyes.

The next day was Saturday, or "Lana-day," as Aster liked to call it now. When they finished the small pile of mail that had come since Thursday, Lana said, "Tell me another story about your mother."

Aster thought a moment. "One day when she was in middle school, she took a fancy to some swirly lead pencils she saw in Woolworth's. She'd already spent all her allowance on candy—Gran said I got my sweet tooth from her—so she helped herself to a couple of pencils and slipped them in her book bag." Aster raised her hand to ward off Lana's disapproval. "No, no, wait. It ate at her. Nobody would have known, but she never could bring herself to use those pencils. A few days later, the manager caught her putting them back. Of course he called Gran, and Mama got a thrashing, but Gran said really, Mama taught herself her own lesson."

"That she did," Lana said. "A very important lesson, too. Even if you do something wrong, it's never too late to try to make it right."

Suddenly Aster realized what she had to do. She took a deep breath. "Lana, can you keep a secret?"

Lana regarded Aster for a long moment. "Secrets are burdens, dear. Sharing them only adds to someone else's load, unless there is something that can be done. Can something be done to make your secret less of a burden?"

Aster thought about that. "I hope so. But I need somebody to help me work it out." She grimaced. "I don't know. I don't want you to be disappointed in me."

"It sounds as if you are disappointed in yourself, my dear. Why don't you tell me what's troubling you, and we'll see what can be done. The important thing is how you go forward."

So Aster began to pour out the whole story: how she was captivated by Ricky's brash assurance and wild, charming ways, and excited to be part of his grand plan to make a fortune and live the high life. "He talked me into selling my daddy's house and investing the money in his schemes. I was so stupid; thank God Daddy set up his life insurance so even I couldn't change the annuity. It's not much, but without it I'd be in a world of hurt now." Aster gave a remorseful shake of her head. "Daddy saw right through Ricky. All of those brilliant ideas were just smoke and mirrors." She paused. "That's not the worst, though."

Lana waited. "Go on, dear."

"Ricky started stealing things," Aster finally said. "No, that's not right—we started stealing things. I don't know, he made it sound like a lark. Robin Hood and Maid Marion, Bonnie and Clyde—" Aster gave a pained laugh "—except look how they ended up. I'd like to say I got smart, but I only got lucky. The night the cops caught him I had cramps, so he was by himself. I didn't get smart until after he went to jail. That's when I realized I didn't like who I was any more. So I divorced him."

Lana looked puzzled. "It sounds like you did exactly the right thing, dear. And now you are making a new life for yourself."

"Except that Ricky's out of jail and says I owe him because I was his partner and he never ratted on me. He says he's going to tell everybody that I was a thief, too, unless I give him money. He's been following me. He knows about Andrew, and about you. Last Saturday he was in Angelo's parking lot and I don't know what would have happened if Corey hadn't decked him."

"Our Corey? Hit someone?"

Aster perked up a little. "Not exactly hit, Lana. Ricky was threatening me; Corey drove by and stopped. When he came over, Ricky called him some names and poked him. Corey whipped him over on his back, right there in the parking lot." Aster laughed at Lana's astonishment. "Turns out our 'Our Corey' has a black belt."

"My gracious. Good for Corey," Lana said. "But Ricky is now angry, and will return." Aster nodded. Lana sat back in her chair and drummed her fingers on the desk. "How much money does he want?"

"A thousand dollars."

"I presume you know that's just the beginning. He will want more."

Aster gave a glum nod. She said softly, "There were some robberies that were never solved, and he says I can either pay up or go back to jail with him. Or team up with him again." She shivered. "As if that's going to happen."

"I doubt he could prove anything," Lana said. "Unless, of course, you have some of the stolen property." Lana frowned at Aster, who lowered her eyes, ashamed.

"Ricky gave me an emerald ring," Aster said. "I'm pretty sure it was stolen. But it was like Mama's pencils; I've never been able to wear it."

Lana peered at the clock on her desk. "We will go get it. You and I are going to the police."

*****

Officer Tobias Mitchell, a lean man in his mid-forties with a ginger crewcut, met Aster and Lana in the lobby of the imposing new police station on Jefferson Avenue.

"My friend is being blackmailed," Lana said. She nodded at Aster, who gave the policeman a tentative smile.

Officer Mitchell led them over to a table and pulled out a small notebook. "Your full name?" he said to Aster.

"Aster Elizabeth Bloom."

He looked up in surprise. "You're Miranda Ridgeway's granddaughter. My granny knew yours. You might remember her. Emily Kirkam?"

Aster brightened. "Of course I remember Emily. She and Gran used to can up a storm every August. Lordy, it got some kind of hot in that kitchen. How is Emily?"

"Her heart finally gave out last year, but she was feisty to the last. I remember she always kept a big ol' photo on her bookcase of her and Miranda when they were little."

"I have that same photo," Aster exclaimed. "They were so adorable in those frilly white dresses and little black Mary Janes." Aster felt a pang of regret, wishing she had kept up with Emily. Suddenly, she ached to know more about what Gran was like as a girl.

Lana looked pointedly at her watch and cleared her throat. Aster and Officer Mitchell took the hint. "I heard that Ricky got out," he said, "so I assume this has something to do with him. We were all real sorry when you got mixed up with his crowd."

"Not nearly as sorry as I am," Aster said. "Yeah, first thing after he got out, Ricky came wanting a thousand dollars. I don't have that kind of money."

Officer Mitchell wrote something in his notebook. "How does he communicate with you?"

"He met me outside my apartment and then in Angelo's parking lot. Last time he gave me his phone number; I'm supposed to call him as soon as I have the money. He's been following me. I'm afraid he might do something to Lana here, or one of my other friends."

"Has he threatened to harm you? If he has, we can get a restraining order."

"No, not exactly. But he, um," Aster hesitated. She glanced at Lana. "Ricky got me to help him with some of the robberies, and he says he could put me in jail too."

Aster remembered the ring. She reached into her purse. "Here. I'm pretty sure this ring was stolen."

Officer Mitchell took the ring and inspected it. "I'll check this against the database of stolen property."

Lana spoke. "If it's not on the list, then it's just his word against hers; correct, Officer?"

"I can't really say, Ma'am." Officer Mitchell scratched his head. He looked at Aster. "I wonder if Ricky had anything to do with last week's robbery in Hidenwood."

"What kinds of things were taken?" Aster said.

"Mostly cash and jewelry. No electronics or artwork, and these people had plenty."

Aster sighed. "That sounds like Ricky. His fence for jewelry and silver went to jail too, but he might be out, or maybe Ricky found somebody else."

Officer Mitchell passed his notebook and pen over to Aster. "Write down your address, phone number and email. Write down Ricky's phone number, too." When she finished, he snapped the notebook closed and stood up. "I have an idea, but I need to check it out. In the meantime, keep your cell phone charged and don't hesitate to call 911 if anything looks suspicious. Be careful."

Two days later, on Monday afternoon, Aster was in Hilton Village making deliveries when her phone rang. "Miss Bloom, it's Tobias Mitchell from the Newport News police. We have a plan I'd like to discuss with you."

Chapter Six

The next evening, Aster's fingers were shaking so much that she had to retype the text message several times. Officer Mitchell's solid presence next to her at the table in the interrogation room made her feel safe, at least for now. Finally he gave her a thumbs-up and Aster pressed "Send." She dropped the phone on the table and leaned against the back of the hard metal chair, every muscle tight with anxiety. Aster closed her eyes and pretended to be Lana: cool, assured, certain.

Her phone burbled and Aster jumped. They both leaned over and checked the display. "That's Ricky," Aster said, her voice hardly more than a whisper. She couldn't bring herself to touch the phone, so Officer Mitchell brought up Ricky's reply. They read his text together.

"We're on," said Officer Mitchell. "You'll be fine. We'll be right there with you."

An hour later, Aster waited for a free spot, then sat down on one of the sofas near the fireplace in Patrick Henry Mall's food court. With only ten shopping days until Christmas, the mall was packed with holiday shoppers. She knew that Officer Mitchell was among the shoppers, and it was all she could do not to look around for him. She raised her hand to pat the tiny wireless microphone pinned in her bra, then thought better of it. Instead, she slid her hands under her thighs and pressed her fingers into the sofa's smooth fake leather.

Ricky appeared in front of her. He glared at the boy and the woman who shared her sofa; the woman hastily grabbed the boy's arm and hurried off. Aster slid her hands out from under her legs. She had to be ready.

Ricky settled down next to her. Remembering her script, Aster resisted the urge to scoot away from him. She gave him a big smile. "You got the money?" he said.

"In my purse." Ricky reached down to the floor for Aster's bag, but she kicked it to her other side.

"Not so fast," she said in a teasing voice. "What did you bring me?" She held out her hand and pasted an expectant, almost flirtatious expression on her face.

Responding as she hoped he would, Ricky's bravado softened into playfulness. "Oh, you'll like these, cutie," he said, reaching into his pocket. He looked around, then brought out his hand and opened his fist. "These are real. Not like that dumb emerald."

Aster stifled a gasp. The tennis bracelet and ring in Ricky's hand were so beautiful, she almost forgot her script. "God, Ricky, that tennis bracelet's gorgeous." She touched it. "Look at the size of those diamonds. I love the way the gold twists around them, making those little hearts." She picked up the ring. "Wow, this ring is amazing. That's the biggest, roundest opal I've ever seen. With diamonds all around it." She slipped it on her finger and held it out for him to admire. "Look, it fits." She brought it in for closer inspection. "Whoa, are those emeralds on the sides?"

Ricky preened. "I figured you'd like them." He watched her admire the jewels. "You're really my same little cutie, aren't you, Aster." Aster gave him a wistful smile, then let her gaze drift over to the fireplace. "We had some good times," Ricky said. "And I know we could have a lot more." He took her hand and folded her fingers around the bracelet. "If you marry me, you'll have all the pretty things you want. We'll be rich."

Aster looked at Ricky in astonishment. *This dumbass actually fell for it,* she thought. And there was something about the way he said "If you marry me" that made her feel strong. Suddenly she wasn't afraid any more.

A burly hand clamped onto Ricky's shoulder from behind. Officer Mitchell came around the sofa and intoned, "Richard Esterbrook, you are under arrest for grand larceny." He nodded at Aster. "Good job," he said. "Your descriptions were a bang-on match for the database."

*****

It was almost midnight by the time the police had everything they needed from her. Feeling pleased with herself, not to mention relieved, Aster desperately needed to crow about what she had done, but there was no one she could call at this hour without scaring them to death first. She took out her phone. *Maybe I'll text Corey and see if he's up.* But she realized she didn't have his number. Frustrated, she went to bed and turned out the light. Half an hour later, she got up and opened a Stephanie Plum book. If she couldn't sleep, at least she could laugh.

*****

First thing the next morning, Aster called Winnie.

"Hey, Aster, hang on," Winnie said. Aster heard her call, "Bye, Ben, love you," then, "So, 'sup, girlfriend? You're usually still snoring at this hour."

Aster launched into her story. But at Aster's first mention of the word "police," Winnie stopped her. "Are you okay? Do I need to drop my Pop-Tart and rush to your rescue?" Aster assured her she was fine. "Good. Then come for supper tonight," Winnie said. "This sounds way too juicy for the phone. And Ben will want to hear it straight from you. He claims I garble things."

When she got to the shop, Margaret was on the phone and a customer was waiting, so Aster quickly shed her coat and got to work. Every time there was a lull where Aster started to say something to Margaret about last night, the phone rang or someone walked in and Margaret said, "Hold that thought, Aster." Aster felt she would burst wide open if she had to hold it in for even two more minutes. At least there was a delivery scheduled for a Bay Haven resident that afternoon; only the knowledge that she would be able to tell Lana kept her from exploding.

Karin was working the reception desk at Bay Haven when Aster signed in, so she left the delivery, hurried up to Lana's apartment, and rang the bell.

"Come in," Lana called.

"It's locked, Lana," Aster said. She heard Lana grunt with effort, then the creak of the walker. The door opened wide.

"Aster! What a lovely surprise. Come in, my dear."

"Lana, I have so much to tell you. The police called me and I helped them arrest Ricky last night." Aster followed Lana over to the sofa.

Lana's face lit up with delight. "Slow down, dear. Tell me everything."

"Well, the policeman we talked to called me Monday and said they could use my help to find out if Ricky had done that robbery over in Hidenwood. So yesterday I went back and he helped me send Ricky a text. I pretended I wanted Ricky to give me something pretty in exchange for the money. It turns out that emerald ring he gave me wasn't stolen, but it was fake, Lana, not even worth fifty dollars." Aster saw the question in Lana's eyes. "Uh huh, that's good; that means I'm not in trouble for those old robberies. Anyway, I got all annoyed about the fake ring in my text and told Ricky I had his money, but in exchange I wanted something real."

"Did you have the money?" Lana said.

"I guess so—the police gave me a thick envelope. They even had me wear a wire, just like on the cop shows! And I had to study pictures of the stolen jewelry and learn what to say so they could identify them." Aster grinned, enjoying herself immensely. "It worked; Ricky brought a gorgeous diamond bracelet and an opal ring, and I said, 'Ooh, a diamond bracelet. I love how the gold wraps around them, making little hearts.' Officer Mitchell said I described it perfectly. He arrested Ricky and took him away in handcuffs, right there in the food court at Patrick Henry Mall."

Lana clapped her hands. "I wish I could have been there. I am so proud of you, Aster."

"I have you to thank, Lana. You got me there. And you know, when I was in the police station, waiting for Ricky to text me back, I pretended I was you. That helped me feel calm and strong."

"You flatter me, Aster, but I am pleased to hear that I helped."

Aster thought a moment. "And then Ricky said something that made me feel—I don't know, angry, maybe?—but suddenly I wasn't afraid of him anymore. He said, 'If you marry me, you'll have all the pretty things you want.'"

"Perhaps you thought, 'I can buy my own pretty things, thank you very much?'"

"Yes!" Aster cried. "Now I remember—the story about your mink coat. Oh, Lana, I have learned so much from you."

*****

That night, after Winnie had pried out every last detail of Aster's story, she jumped up and gave Aster a big hug. "You go, girl. So, did they throw away the key?"

"Just about. He violated probation big time, so they set bail pretty high. Officer Mitchell said nobody's putting up the money for him, not even his mother."

"Good riddance," Winnie said. "So, about this Officer Mitchell?"

Aster laughed. She felt so good, now that she'd told Winnie, that she could forgive her friend anything. "Married," she said.

"Oops," Winnie said, reaching for the plate of Oreos on the kitchen counter.

Ben drawled, "Well, Aster, I sold some insurance to a gentleman this week who might be of some interest to you." He winked. Aster grinned.

"Really, who?" Winnie said as she passed the cookies to Aster. Aster took one, twisted it, and licked the creamy, sugary filling. She smiled; Oreos always reminded her of Gran's milk and cookies after school.

"Fellow by the name of Edgar Samuelson," Ben said. "Widower with no children. Beneficiary is some charity."

"He sounds perfect!" Winnie exclaimed. Aster and Ben shook with laughter. "What?" she said, looking from one to the other.

"Mr. Samuelson is on the far side of ninety," Ben said, chuckling. "He's over at Bay Haven."

"And he's been after Lana since she got there," Aster added. "She can't stand him."

"Oops," said Winnie.

On Saturday, Corey was hurt that Aster had waited so long to tell him about Ricky. "You could've told me, Aster. We're friends, aren't we? You know I would've had your back."

"I thought about it, Corey, really I did. But it was something I needed to handle on my own. I know you'd be an awesome bodyguard."

Corey glowered. "You couldn't afford me. I charge at least a dollar a day."

Aster laughed. "Yeah, well, I was afraid to get anyone else involved. I was even afraid to tell Lana, but I'm glad I did. She dragged my butt down to the police station, and now I feel like I have my life back." She sipped her latte. "I started to text you that night after it was all over, but we've never exchanged numbers."

Corey slapped his forehead. "Yeah," Aster said, "That's about what I did." She brought out her phone. "I got so used to just seeing you on Saturdays... how about let's fix that right now."

"Speaking of getting your life back," Corey said, after he tapped Aster's number into his phone, "what are you doing for Christmas?"

Aster tensed. The holidays were the only times that her proud independence had faltered these last few years. Christmas was family time. Ben and Winnie had done their best to make her feel welcome the last two Christmases, but they were going to Ben's family in Roanoke this year. She had put off thinking about it.

"I honestly don't know," she said. But suddenly she remembered one of Gran's favorite sayings: "The best cure for lonesome is to get out there and do something nice for somebody." Aster brightened. "I suppose, something with Lana."

"I talked to my Mom, and she'd like to invite both you and Lana to our house on Christmas Day."

Corey's unexpected invitation flooded Aster with gratitude and relief. "Oh, Corey, that's so sweet, thank you." Her heart leapt at the idea of buying presents for more than just Winnie and Ben. "How old are your sisters?"

Chapter 7

On Christmas Day, Aster parked in the driveway of a tidy ranch house on Turlington Avenue and helped Lana up the walk. Before they reached the front stoop, the door flung open and Corey came out. Between them, Corey and Aster got Lana up the two steps to the door, where a pair of teenage girls hovered.

While Corey made the introductions, a tall woman with a salt and pepper bob came down the hall, wiping her hands on an apron that proclaimed, "If Mama Ain't Happy, Ain't Nobody Happy." Aster liked her already.

"My Gran had that very same apron," she said.

"I wore my first one slam out," Mrs. Norcross said, enveloping Aster in a warm hug, then extending her hand to Lana. "Imogen Norcross, but please call me Norrie."

After that, the day went from better to best. Norrie was a fabulous cook, and opening presents was a laugh-filled, joyous time. It ended too soon. At three o'clock, Lana apologetically pleaded exhaustion and asked Aster to take her home.

Corey walked them out to the car. "Thank you both for coming. Mom loves to cook, but my sisters are always on some kind of a diet and—" he patted his middle "—Lord knows I need to watch mine. You gave her a reason to pull out all the stops."

"This was a wonderful day," Lana said. "I haven't had such a fine Christmas since, well…" She paused, and her voice faded. "…well, it's been a very, very long time." She reached for Corey's hand and held it between both her gloved hands. "Thank you. And thank your dear mother again, too."

After helping Lana into the car, Corey carefully closed the door, then turned to Aster. "Not to press my luck or anything, but could we maybe do something New Year's Eve?"

Aster hadn't thought as far ahead as New Year's Eve. For the last two years she had fended off Winnie's perfect dates and gone to bed early with a pillow over her head, ridiculing the idiots who crammed into crowded spaces that were either too hot (clubs) or too cold (Times Square). People who spent too much money and drank themselves silly, all for the privilege of watching the clock tick over. But suddenly she couldn't think of anything better. What was happening to her carefully-crafted independence? "I'd love to," she said.

On Saturday, the day after Christmas, Lana was thrilled to hear that Aster was going out with Corey. "Tell me, what will you wear?" Lana said, her gaze drifting down to Aster's distressed blue jeans and dirty Adidas's. Aster laughed. "I do have some nice clothes, Lana. I'm thinking I'll wear a black skirt with a sparkly top. Maybe put my hair up." To demonstrate, Aster used her hands to pile her hair on top of her head.

"Very nice," Lana said. "There's nothing lovelier than a girl who takes care with her appearance." *She is a sly one*, Aster thought. Lana was always immaculately dressed, coiffed and made up. *Okay, it won't kill me to make a little effort to dress up for her.*

"Describe your top," Lana said. "What kind of neckline does it have?"

"Kind of a scoop," Aster said, drawing her finger in a broad arc across her chest.

"Excellent," Lana said. "Come with me." She led Aster over to her dresser. "Open the top drawer." Lana reached in the back and brought out a narrow oblong box, covered in red silk brocade. She handed it to Aster. "This will go well with your sparkly top."

Aster opened the box and drew out a necklace of perfect, graduated pearls. "Oh, Lana, I couldn't possibly…"

"Of course you can. It will please me no end to think of you wearing my pearls. This is as much for me as it is for you."

*****

The booming beat almost made the sidewalk vibrate outside the night club on New Year's Eve. Corey had told Aster that he knew somebody who knew somebody, and had managed to snag two seats at a table. Aster marveled at Corey—he was a constant source of surprises. He turned out to be a good dancer, too, but perhaps that was not so surprising, considering his black belt. All evening, she tried to remember every detail for Lana, starting with the admiration on Corey's face when he picked her up, then the way he had touched his finger lightly to Lana's necklace and said with awe, "They're beautiful. They make your face glow."

When Corey took her in his arms for a slow dance, Aster relaxed, feeling the strength in his arms and his confidence as he guided her around the floor. It didn't matter that he was only an inch or two taller than she; they fit together well. Aster suppressed a giggle, remembering how she had thought Corey was sort of dumpy-looking when she first met him. When he drew her close, she rested her cheek against his.

*****

Two days later, Corey's face broke into a wide grin as soon as Aster came through the sliding doors. She blushed, feeling again his New Year's kiss and the warmth that had poured all the way down to her toes.

"Saturday, January 2," she wrote in the visitors' book. A brand new year—she hoped it would be a good one. Corey reached over and laid his hand on hers. "I had the best time New Year's," he said.

"Me too," Aster said, feeling giddy.

Upstairs, as usual, the door was open and Lana waited at her desk. Aster returned Lana's pearls and told her everything she could remember about the evening.

"He kissed you, I assume?" Lana said.

Aster flushed. "Of course. It was New Year's." Before Lana could ask, she said, "And yes, I liked it. A lot."

After they went through the mail, Lana asked Aster to find her will. "I always review it on the first of the year, in case I want to make some changes," she said. "You will find it in that file box, over by the window."

Out of habit, before she lifted the lid off the file box, Aster looked out the window and surveyed the harbor.

"Oh, Lana, come quickly, you have to see this." Aster rushed over, helped Lana to her feet and escorted her to the window.

A naval ship was gliding through Hampton Roads channel out toward the Bay. Sailors at attention rimmed its decks. Unconsciously, Aster stood at attention. "Isn't this wonderful, Lana? Every time I see one of these great ships sail, I feel so proud, and ... I don't know, unworthy, somehow."

When Lana didn't respond, Aster turned and was shocked to see tears streaming down the old woman's smooth cheeks. "Lana! What's wrong? Come, sit down." Aster urged her to the sofa.

"No." Lana shook her head violently. "No. I must stay." She took a handkerchief from the pouch on her walker and dabbed her eyes. The ship proceeded, and the two women, one old, one young, watched until it turned at Thimble Shoals Light and headed out to sea.

"I send them to myself," Lana said.

"What?" Aster said, mystified.

"The flowers. Every month. I send them to myself." Lana stood fixed, staring after the ship. "I have lived a memory instead of a life."

"How can you say that," Aster cried. "You've had a wonderful life, Lana." Aster was shaken. She admired Lana's independence and, for her own sake, wanted to believe that Lana had been happy and fulfilled.

"I stood right there," Lana said quietly, pointing at a spot on the lawn beneath them, "when the Enterprise sailed. It was January second, 1939. I was fifteen years old. Terry was eighteen. I picked out one of the sailors on deck and pretended it was Terry. I just about dislocated my shoulder, waving."

Terry. "T". Aster held her breath, willing Lana to continue.

Lana's words flowed, as if a locked door had been forced open. "Terry—Terrence—lived up the street from me in Hilton Village. His father and mine worked at the shipyard. His sister Brenda and I were best friends from when we were toddlers." Lana paused, then said flatly, "Brenda got the flu and died when we were fourteen."

Aster whispered, "I'm so sorry, Lana." She put her hand on Lana's, where it gripped the walker. "Come, please sit with me." Lana allowed Aster to help her to the sofa.

"Brenda's parents never got over her death," Lana said. "They started blaming themselves, then each other. Terry started spending more and more time at our house, with my brother. Oh, he was a tease, that Terry. He always called me Liliana, and we used to play a silly game called 'If You Marry Me.' Lana clasped her hands in her lap and smiled at Aster. "He'd say things like, 'If you marry me, I'll take you to the top of Mount Everest,' and I'd say, 'If you marry me, I'll race you to the top of Mount Everest.' I always had to do him one better, and he liked to egg me on.

"Terry joined the Navy as soon as he was old enough, and we all stood down there—" Lana gestured toward the window "—when he sailed, the day after New Year's. Oh, how I cried. I was only fifteen, but I already knew Terry was the one." Lana brushed away a tear. "We wrote almost every day. He doodled the prettiest flowers on his letters." Lana's voice became softer, dreamier, with a hint of the South. "He said, 'If you marry me, I'll give you flowers every day.'"

Aster wondered where Terry was now. But she had the sense to stay quiet.

"He came home on leave every chance he could, and we spent just about every minute with each other. When the Enterprise was sent to Hawaii, I started saving my babysitting money, then got an after-school job in a bakery. It about killed me that he was seeing Hawaii without me. The spring before I graduated high school, he came back for two weeks and asked me to marry him." Lana twisted her handkerchief in her hands. "But he didn't get leave again until Christmas, and by then it was too late."

Aster thought, *After 1939... Hawaii. Oh no.* She laid her hand on Lana's knee and said gently, "Pearl Harbor?"

Lana nodded. "He'd just been transferred to the Oklahoma." Aster patted Lana's knee, feeling sad and helpless.

Lana raised her head and stared at the wall. "My family disowned me."

"Why on earth?" Aster cried. "Didn't they love Terry too?"

"Oh, they did, but you see, I got pregnant, and back then, there was no greater disgrace."

"But you were getting married!"

"I wasn't married. That's all that mattered. As soon as I started to show, my family packed me off to the Evangeline Booth home in Richmond and told everybody I'd gone to take care of my aunt in Montana. Even my brother turned on me, and he'd been Terry's best friend. He told Terry he'd better find another best man."

"Did Terry know about the baby?"

"Oh my, yes. He was thrilled. They tried to keep us from each other but we wrote every day, and he started sending me bouquets at the home every month. Oh, I was the envy of all the other girls. He said he couldn't wait for Christmas. I told him, 'If you marry me, we'll have an instant family.'" Lana chuckled.

"And then, Pearl Harbor. I was frantic. I didn't know anything for two weeks. More of Terry's letters came, but nothing after the one dated December 6. I learned that he'd been killed when they sent me the partial letter they found with his things." With both hands, Lana held the handkerchief to her eyes for a moment. "Little Brenda, then Terry. It destroyed his parents. They wouldn't even acknowledge that I was carrying their son's child. I suppose they were already too far gone with the drink."

Lana's eyes brimmed with glistening tears. "I couldn't even go to his funeral. I was eight months pregnant and the home said it wasn't safe for me to travel. I always thought they'd been told not to let me go. Terry's last bouquet arrived on December seventeenth. A month later, I gave birth. I never knew if it was a boy or a girl. They told me it was healthy, and promised me that it was going to a good family."

Aster began to cry. "Oh, Lana, how awful for you."

"Now, don't you start, darling girl. Lord knows I've cried enough tears for both of us."

Aster wiped her eyes with the backs of her hands.

"Please use a tissue, dear." Lana said. Aster obediently reached for the box on the end table.

When Aster had recovered, she ventured to ask, "So that's when you went to New York?"

"Yes. There was nothing left for me in Virginia. I changed my name and went North to college and career. I would have liked to marry, but I never met another man who made me feel the way Terry did."

Aster had a thought. "So when that European count said, 'If you marry me, I'll buy you a mink coat'—?"

"He couldn't know, but it wasn't his game to play," Lana said. "And as soon as I could afford it, I started sending myself flowers every month. I told myself I was keeping Terry's promise. Men thought I was very mysterious, that I had a secret lover." Lana turned to Aster. "But really, I was building a barrier around myself, Aster. I walled off all the sorrow and the pain, and clung to the only good thing I knew for sure: that Terry loved me. I kept his memory alive with flowers, and I guarded against ever being hurt. I never allowed myself to love again."

Aster struggled to process Lana's confession, which contradicted everything she thought she had known, and admired, about her friend. "Didn't you ever try to look for your child?"

Lana looked at Aster with a rueful smile. "I thought about it, all the time. Oh, how I longed to see my child grow up; to see the person he or she would become. But I was afraid I wouldn't be strong enough to deal with the gossip."

Aster raised her eyebrows. "Lana, I've never met anyone as strong as you are. Except maybe my Gran."

"I was tainted by my upbringing, dear. A single woman, successful in a man-dominated world—I struggled every day to prove myself, and if they found out that I'd had a child out of wedlock, well, it could easily have ruined my career. By the time society came around to accepting such things, I was already an old lady."

Lana gave a quavery sigh. "I never should have burdened you with this, my dear Aster. And I will appreciate your keeping it in confidence. Please, store it away as a lesson from your old friend." She took Asters hands in both of hers. "Don't shut people out, darling. Don't hide from love."

Aster didn't know what to say. She had too much to think about.

"Do you remember what I told you, about not sharing secrets unless there is something to be done?" Lana said. Aster nodded, mute, and Lana continued. "Well, there is something you can do. Actually, you have already done it. Since you came into my life, I like to pretend that I had a daughter, and she was just like you."

Chapter 8

"Earth to Aster," Corey called, just before she reached the lobby's automatic glass doors. Her reverie interrupted, Aster turned and saw Corey with his hands spread, palms up. "Hello? Coffee?" he said.

Aster gave herself a mock head-smack. "Sorry, my mind's a zillion miles away."

"Ya think?" Corey's voice was teasing, but there was a hint of caution in his eyes. "So, what happened? Did Miss Rachman convince you I'm not good enough for you?"

"Oh my, no," Aster said. She hurried over to the counter, remembering Lana's words—*Don't shut people out, darling.* "Just the opposite. She told me some stuff about her childhood and warned me not to shut people out. Like I just did to you. Sorry."

Corey reached over the counter and took Aster's hand. "You can try to shut me out, but it won't change anything." He took a deep breath. "I don't want to rush you, but I know how I feel, and it's up to you how you take it—with a bucket or an umbrella." Without waiting for Aster's response, he turned and reached for his coat behind the office door.

Aster opened her mouth, then closed it. A memory leapt into her mind. "So that's what she meant," she said with wonder.

"What who meant?" said Corey, returning with his coat.

"Sometimes when I got cranky and squirmy, Gran used to call me her 'little umbrella girl.' I never knew what she meant. Until now." Entwining her arm around Corey's when he came around the end of the counter, Aster matched her step to his. "Bucket," she proclaimed happily.

*****

That night, Aster's mind ricocheted between delicious thoughts of Corey and revisiting every detail of Lana's story. Lana's revelation that her independence had been a brittle facade forced Aster to rethink her own path. She had worked so hard to be strong, and become so accustomed to keeping her distance from people that, like Lana, she was afraid to risk being vulnerable. But Lana said, "Don't hide from love."

Lana and Terry were once as happy as Corey and I am, she thought, wishing there were something more she could do for Lana. Well, at least I can be the best friend I know how to be.

As she undressed before bed, Aster looked fondly at the cardboard box on the floor of her closet, as she did every evening. But tonight she took a second look. The box contained her family; in it were photos, her mother's teen diary, and other papers that Gran had saved for her. Aster hadn't looked at its contents since her father died; it had been too painful. But now she was drawn to the box, feeling a need to reconnect. She hoisted it onto her bed and lifted the lid.

An hour later she was still at it, looking at the pictures, letters and diary with new eyes, as if she were showing and reading each one to Lana and Corey. She started a little pile of things to show them: her parents' wedding picture, the love note her father wrote when Aster was born, the picture of Gran and Emily as young girls. Finally she came to the large, tan envelope at the bottom of the box, marked "Legal Documents." Aster remembered sliding her father's death certificate into this envelope. She picked it up, held it against her chest for a long moment, then undid the clasp.

Inside, she found the death certificates for her father, mother and grandmother. Under them was her own birth certificate: Aster Elizabeth, born to Edward and Christine Bloom, July 15, 1990. And her mother's: Christine Evelyn, born to Miranda and Robert Ridgeway, November 5, 1965. Aster handled the precious documents gingerly, careful not to damage the fragile pages.

When she went to slide the papers back in the envelope, they got stuck on something. She removed them, peered inside for the obstruction, and fished out a smaller envelope she had never seen before. On it, written in a swirly hand she didn't recognize, were the words, *Birth Cert – Save*. The once-white envelope was sealed with yellowed tape that crumbled when Aster lifted the flap. Inside were two pieces of paper. She unfolded one of them: Female Booker, born Richmond, Virginia, January 17, 1942. Mother: Lorna Booker. Father: unknown. *Who's this?* Aster thought. *It's not Gran—her parents were William and Martha Maxwell.*

But when Aster unfolded the second document, her mouth fell open. She knew she would not sleep that night.

The next morning, a Sunday, she forced herself to wait until ten o'clock before rushing over to Bay Haven. She signed in quickly, giving Karin a wave—Corey was off on Sundays. Upstairs, Lana was just finishing her breakfast and Janine was making the bed when Aster burst into the apartment.

"Aster, dear child, whatever is the matter?" Lana cried, alarmed.

"Nothing, I hope," Aster said, out of breath. She sat down and leaned forward. "Lana, listen to me carefully." She waited while Lana set down her toast. "Was your name ever Lorna Booker?"

All of the color drained from Lana's face. Her hands fluttered; Aster took them in her own. "Where did you hear that?" Lana whispered.

"I found some papers, Lana. One of them is a birth certificate for a Female Booker, born to Lorna Booker on January 17, 1942."

Lana's entire body trembled. Aster looked to alert Janine, but Lana gripped Aster's hands, hard. "A girl. I had a little girl," she said. A wavering smile brought a hint of color back to her face. "Tell me, how did you get this paper? Was there anything else with it?"

"It was in a box in my closet. With an adoption certificate." In a voice overflowing with emotion, Aster said, "Lana, your daughter was my Gran."

A Different Kind of
Christmas

Narielle Living

Chapter 1

Hope stood and stretched; her hands dirty from the soil. Despite the chill in the air, the afternoon sun was bright, causing her to squint in despair at the fragile patch of garden. Hopefully she had done it right this time. She had spent all morning weeding and spraying soapy water on her plants, nurturing them with water saved in barrels from the rains. She was hoping and praying that something edible grew even this late in the year, but she'd never had to try to grow food in the winter before. Her late summer garden had been a dismal failure. What did she know about farming or food? For that matter, what did she know about starting her whole world over?

Absently wiping sweat from her forehead, she tried not to panic about her dwindling supply of rations. Most people couldn't use the grocery stores anymore, never mind any of the other luxuries from what she thought of as "back then." *Never mind*, she decided. *No sense wasting time longing for the past when the present has so many troubles.*

"Mommy, do you need any help?" Sandy, her six-year-old daughter, walked into the backyard holding a bucket. Hope smiled, trying to hide her weariness. Her ten-year-old son Jared, silent as a shadow, stood behind his sister.

"Thanks, guys, but I think I'm okay for now. Everything's taken care of. You can play for a little while, but later this afternoon I'll need help starting the fire for supper." Watching them start to wander toward the front yard, she held her tongue. They were good kids, and they knew the rules. Besides, this was probably one of the last warm days they'd have for a while. November in this part of Virginia was odd, it could be warm one day and freezing the next. But for her the weather wasn't the problem, letting go of the constant fear that something else was going to happen was the difficult part.

Sandy turned and looked at her. "I'll be up in the tree," Sandy said solemnly.

Hope sighed. She wasn't sure what to do about this behavior, or if she should do anything at all. "Okay, honey, you go ahead. Just be careful climbing into the lookout."

Jared's gaze was piercing as he stared at his mother. She felt the heat of anger coming off him. Just as she didn't know what to do with Sandy, she had no idea how to handle Jared. Some days she thought about giving up, but that wasn't a real option. She refused to be defeated by the circumstances.

"You shouldn't let her do that, you know," he spoke defiantly. "Dad's not coming back, and you shouldn't let her think he is."

"We don't know that for certain, honey. We don't even know what happened to him, so there's always hope." She spoke quietly, trying to offer some measure of reassurance to a son that had to grow up so quickly.

"C'mon, Mom, he left to go find food and whatever, but we know what's out there. He probably got beaten and left to die somewhere. You've gotta stop kidding yourself."

Birdsong erupted behind her, and for just a moment Hope closed her eyes, almost able to lull herself into believing everything was as it had been before. She could almost do it, too. The sun was warm against her face, and the stillness of the neighborhood was typical of any suburban area. The middle class homes stood solid and reassuring, homes where families ate together and laughed together. Homes where phones rang constantly, relatives visited and neighbors dropped by to say hello. They lived in a neighborhood with nice houses and no crime, a great place to raise the kids. The grass was always mowed, flower gardens were lovingly tended, and people always waved in greeting.

Until it all collapsed. When the financial crisis loomed, everyone shrugged it off. "This has happened before, we'll get through it," was the collective thought. Everyone watched as Europe teetered and fell over the precipice of disaster, and tried to ignore what was happening. After all, a great big ocean separated Europe from the United States. But instead of recovery, an international economic collapse occurred this past spring. Banks closed, real estate lost all value, and stock markets around the world were a joke.

Hope supposed it had been inevitable and they had all missed the warning signs, but she, like most everyone else, was taken completely by surprise. Once the United States fell, despair loomed worldwide. The people of the United States, used to modern comforts, struggled to survive this new catastrophe.

Hope could never have predicted a situation like this. On television, sure, because that wasn't real. But in Yorktown, Virginia, it hardly seemed possible.

Spring stretched into summer and then fall and now winter; nothing got better. They no longer had fuel to drive the cars. The electricity had gone out in August. Computers sat gathering dust while refrigerators were used as storage for whatever could be picked, gathered, or grown. Squirrels and rabbits, once constant garden nuisances, were now in short supply. And husbands went off to try to find food and information and never came home. Hope sighed in frustration, feeling a pain in her chest.

If only I hadn't let him leave by himself, if only we knew back then that nobody should go out alone...

She forced her thoughts away from the past and tried to focus on what she needed in the moment. *Maybe we can gather the leaves and use them in fires. We've got enough leaves in the yard now.*

Jared continued to stare at her as her thoughts raced. "I know you think your sister is wasting her time, but right now she needs to be up there looking for Dad. It makes her feel better to think she's on lookout for him. This is just as hard for her as it is for you, sweetie."

"Mom! Jared!" Jared and Hope jumped, startled by the tone in Sandy's voice. "Mr. Conway is here."

As she hurried to the front yard, Hope felt a moment of unrest. She always had that feeling when Marty Conway stopped at their house. An ex-army officer, Marty had taken on patrol responsibility and security for the neighborhood. During the day he could be seen riding his bike, armed and in uniform, watching for any sign of trouble from the outsiders. The whistle he carried acted as a first alert that someone was in trouble. Hope wondered if he had any news for them. *At least he hasn't used the whistle*, Hope thought morosely. The only time he had used the whistle was to alert the neighborhood when her husband had gone missing.

She hated the whistle.

Forcing a smile to her face, Hope raised a hand in greeting as she stepped into the front yard. "Hi, Marty, how are things?"

Marty nodded. "Hi Hope, kids…"

At forty-five years old, retired for two years, his buzz cut had grown out a bit but he still retained a military posture. Hope admired him for what he did. He had taken over a difficult, almost impossible task, and he never once complained. Marty, along with the team he had put together, made sure that the looting and crime that was rampant in the surrounding counties did not invade the neighborhood. He was thorough and friendly, but she had no doubt that if confronted with a threat he would respond with equal force.

Some level of law still existed, but Marty had told her he didn't put a whole lot of faith in what was out there. Hope remembered his words at the beginning of the collapse. "I don't want to trust the people who are part of an organization linked to the government. We're in this situation because of the government, so why would I have any faith in them?" Although he grudgingly accepted that the government night patrols enforced the recently imposed martial law, he refused to relinquish daytime security and spent his days patrolling the neighborhood. Marty was trained to kill, and Hope knew that in a dangerous situation he would always fire first and ask questions later. She was simultaneously afraid and relieved that he lived near her.

Standing before her, Marty grew silent. Hope knew without having to be told that something was wrong. A sour taste rose in her throat. "Okay, kids, why don't you go in the house and get the fireplace set up for me?"

"I want to stay on lookout," Sandy whined.

Hope hesitated until she saw Marty's slight nod. "Go on in the house, sweetie. I'll be in soon. Maybe after we cook we can play a board game."

"I'll handle lookout for a little while," Marty boomed. At that, Sandy scrambled out of the tree and followed her big brother into the house.

Hope opened her mouth to speak, but the words got caught. *Does he have news? It can't be good, not the way he's looking at me.*

"It's not about your husband. I'm sorry," Marty said.

She knew it was unreasonable, but she couldn't help feeling disappointed. It was probably well past the time that she could expect her husband back, but there was no dislodging the hope from her heart.

"My sources tell me we're about to have another problem." Marty's words were rushed. "I think this one is going to be bad, and there's no telling where it might lead."

"Sources?"

"People I know. We've been communicating on satellite radio."

"Radio?" Hope knew she sounded like an idiot, but she couldn't help it.

"It's the one thing that hasn't gone down. Don't worry, it's from the army and it's secure."

Hope shook her head. Sometimes the bizarre nature of this new world made her feel as if the ground beneath her was no longer solid. "What did your, um, sources tell you?"

Marty looked around discreetly before answering in a quiet voice. "We all know that everything has been shutting down. There's no money, no way to get anywhere, and no real reason to stay if things are bad. Now it's really going to hit the fan."

Hope was confused. "What are you talking about?"

"You know of Eastern State Hospital, right?"

With a sense of dread Hope nodded, uncertain she wanted to hear this.

"Nobody's working. Why go to work when you're not going to get paid?"

"So nobody's there for the patients," Hope said.

Marty nodded. "As of this morning, the patients have all left the building."

Hope swallowed nervously. "But, these are psychiatric patients. Where would they go?"

Marty stared at her with an intensity that was unnerving. "Without medication, who knows what most of those folks are going to do. It's sad, and under normal circumstances I wouldn't be worried about people with mental health issues, but we no longer have normal circumstances. I'd say we're going to have to be prepared for some kind of issue from that group."

Hope shook her head, trying to think clearly. "But Marty—" Hope stopped herself, trying to sort her thoughts before she spoke.

Marty's gaze was direct. "I know what you're thinking, Hope. They're just people, what's the harm, we don't know that they're headed toward us, right?" Hope nodded. "While that is certainly valid, this is still a concern. Plus, we've got other problems we need to discuss. I'm calling a neighborhood meeting tonight at the Warren's house. We've got security issues, and we need to talk about our future."

The constant feeling of dread that had lodged in her stomach tightened. A note of resignation crept into her voice as she asked Marty what time they should be at the meeting.

"Six o'clock sharp. Bring some food; we're going to share what we have. And be ready for some changes, Hope. We've had a security breach on our perimeter and we need to shore up our resources. See you tonight." With a wave he left, no doubt to spread the word about the meeting.

"Mom?"

Hope jumped. Sandy stepped out from behind the dusty, unused car in the driveway. Her eyes were brimming with tears.

"What is it? Are you okay?" Hope went to her and knelt down, wiping the tears from her daughter's face.

"Wh-what did Mr. Conway say? Will Daddy be home for Christmas?"

Hope's arms enveloped her daughter. "No, sweetie, he hasn't seen or heard from your father." The question startled Hope. She hadn't even been thinking about the holidays—how could she? What the hell kind of Christmas would this year bring? She had to somehow balance reality with trying to preserve her children's emotional well-being. "Mr. Conway knows lots of people who are watching for him, and if anyone hears anything Mr. Conway will tell us. Right now all we can do is hope for the best."

She stood for a moment with her arms wrapped around her little girl, trying to offer some measure of comfort. Sandy pulled away. "I'm going inside to play."

Hope watched her walk inside the house, wondering how she was going to be able to protect her children. *Sometimes I think it's not even the physical dangers I need to protect them from as much as all the heartache that's coming our way.*

Taking a deep breath, Hope turned her mind to other pressing matters. Tonight's dinner was her first obstacle. With the scarcity of food, community dinners were always easier. As she thought about what she had on hand to bring, she let out a short laugh. "Good thing I used to shop at the superstores. Buying in bulk was not just economical; it's been a lifesaver for meals. Literally."

She still had rice she could cook, and she could add the few tomatoes and wild onions that she had managed to grow. A pinch of salt and that would feed more than a couple of people. After the collapse, everybody's tastes had changed. Not that long ago most people she knew wouldn't touch a meal that wasn't properly seasoned and without meat. Hunger drove people to eat things they might not have thought possible, including dubious combinations of edible plants and flowers.

Or anything they could get their hands on. She couldn't stop the thread of panic that crept into her thoughts. *What will it be like in the long winter months, once our food supply is gone?*

Chapter 2

Although serious topics were to be discussed at the night's meeting, Hope treated the event as a social occasion. She decided to wear a long black skirt with flat shoes paired with a long-sleeved turquoise silk blouse. Despite the fact that it was November, the weather was still warm. With her long, dark hair pulled back and a hint of makeup to complete the look, Hope felt almost normal. Almost.

For obvious reasons nobody went out anymore; no movies were showing at the cinema and restaurants had all closed down weeks ago. Besides that, there were inherent dangers in going into crowded areas. People were desperate and crime had risen dramatically. Drug addicts needed a fix, people were hungry and thirsty, and the rules of social structure were gone. Safety came first, and safety existed only with known groups of people.

Dusk was falling when the people of the neighborhood gathered at the Warren's house. Marty had told everyone the Warren's was one of the safer homes in the area, since it sat almost in the center of the other homes and streets. To protect the neighborhood, Marty had convinced people who lived on the perimeter to abandon their homes. Once the perimeter was established, the entry and exit points were always guarded. With the population down to just over one hundred people, it was the best they could do.

When Hope and the kids arrived she was surprised to find that there weren't as many people as she expected. Placing her rice dish on the kitchen counter, Hope turned to Sharon Warren and smiled. "Hey, how are you tonight?"

Sharon nodded. "As good as can be expected, I guess. Looks like there won't be as many people joining us tonight."

"Why not?"

"Marty said that about half the neighbors have decided they didn't like how things were going around here. They think we should make an effort to get more guns and take a stronger stance on our security."

"But Marty is tight on security. He doesn't allow strangers to get through and he's the one that originally came up with the idea to secure the neighborhood. What more do these people think we should be doing?"

Sharon shrugged. "I don't really know what they want, but Ed seems to think it's about power for them. Maybe they're looking to start their own little fiefdom or something, where they are in complete control."

Hope shuddered. "This whole thing is surreal. People have lost their minds. Anyway, never mind them. We're better off without them."

Sharon raised a glass of water in salute. "You're right, we are better off without them. Who needs to be surrounded by even more lunatics?"

Hope laughed. "So, how's it going here at home? Are you and Ed getting along okay?"

With a derisive snort, Sharon answered. "Splendidly. Who knew that a national catastrophe could bring us back together? Honestly, Hope, after I found out he was having an affair I thought I could never live with him again. But here I am."

"Here you are," Hope repeated softly. "Sharon, I know this has got to be hard for you, but for what it's worth, I think you're doing the right thing. You put your children and their safety first, and you're all better off here together than scattered around the county with who knows what going on out there."

"You're right, thanks Hope. I'm sorry if I sound selfish, I know that this has got to be difficult for you, too. Have you heard any news about Harlan?"

"No, and with every day that goes by I feel more and more guilty. I should have never let him go out there on his own."

Sharon shook her head. "You didn't know what could happen, none of us knew. It's not your fault."

Hope disagreed. "Both my husband and I should have known better. Neither one of us had any business wandering the streets by ourselves, but for some reason we thought Harlan would be okay out there on his own. He insisted we needed information and he thought he might be able to find us food somewhere. Apparently we were wrong."

Doubt crept into her mind again as it had over the past weeks. Sure, maybe something had happened to Harlan. But she also knew about the rumors. Rumors of him being involved in something shady, rumors of him taking money, rumors of criminal activity. Maybe he really was trying to get back to his home, his family, his life, but the odds were good that the rumors were true. *Nothing I can do about any of this, so I'll continue to push it out of my mind and forget about it. If Harlan makes it back to us then I'll confront him, but until then I can't let the kids know I doubt their father.*

Sharon put an arm around Hope. "Let's hope and pray for the best, okay? In the meantime, come on out in the backyard and enjoy the neighbors. Let's try to have some fun before Marty lays down the new laws for us."

Walking into the backyard, Hope looked around at the neighbors that had gathered. Ruth and Frank, both of them in their early eighties, sat quietly at a wrought iron table on the back deck. Hope knew they both had complicated health problems, but so far they seemed to be holding up just fine. Next to them sat Joan, a single mother of three, content to sit in silence for a few moments while her children swarmed around the large wooden play set. Michael and Corrine Jensen circulated through the crowd, talking to everyone and trying to be upbeat. As grandparents, they used to care for their two toddler grandchildren, but that was no longer the case. She knew they missed their children and grandchildren, but because of what had happened both were wary of venturing out to be with them. Each neighbor had a unique story, and each of them was trying to survive the best they knew how.

Looking across the patio Hope saw Marty staring at her, his blue eyes concerned as he assessed the social situation. With a slight nod at her, he turned to Sharon and said, "I think everyone who wants to be here has arrived. Let's begin."

"Hey, shouldn't we eat first?" Ed called from across the patio.

Marty shook his head. "There will be plenty of time for that after we discuss a couple of things. We're going to need time together to talk, so let me say what I have to say first. We can eat and have further discussion after dinner."

The children drew closer to their parents as a hush settled over the crowd. Marty squared his shoulders and began. "As I have already reported to most of you, we have a situation where the patients at Eastern State Hospital have been released. While this may or may not be a concern for us, we have other security issues that need to be addressed. First, from what I can gather, things in Newberg are rapidly deteriorating. Since it's a more urban environment than here, they don't have the resources we have."

"You mean the wealth of squirrels and rabbits," a voice shouted. Uneasy laughter rippled through the crowd as Marty acknowledged this fact.

"True, they don't have all the furry little creatures that help feed the families in this town. Plus, although troops have been patrolling the streets there is no help for the citizens." Marty hesitated for a moment, glancing at some of the children sitting before him. "Hey kids, why don't you go in the house and start organizing the plates and cups for dinner?" While the younger ones went inside agreeably, some of the older kids stayed to listen. Hope noticed that Jared was one of them.

"Jared," Hope called, "why don't you go help your sister?"

Glaring at his mother, Jared slowly got to his feet and walked toward the house. Hope decided to ignore the fact that he stood just outside the door, waiting to hear what Marty had to say.

Marty noticed, and called out, "You heard your mother, go on in and help your sister. Don't worry, you're really not missing anything. You'll hear all about this and be part of our planning later tonight." Hope nodded her thanks to Marty, watching as Jared quietly slipped inside the house.

Marty turned back to the crowd. "Remember what happened in New Orleans post Katrina? Well, it looks like we've got a situation very similar going on right now, except it's happening in places all over the country."

Ruth called out in a shaky voice, "Marty, what on earth are you talking about?"

He took a breath before continuing. "People can't get their medication, or are starving, or hurt, and the result is that they're dying at a really fast rate. Unfortunately, nobody knows what to do with the bodies in the cities. They have no place to put them. Dead bodies have been put out in the streets and left there, rats crawling all over them. Of course this is going to create more problems down the line."

Frank, who had difficulty hearing, hollered, "When is this mess all going to get straightened out? We live in the greatest country on earth, what in tarnation is happening around here?"

Ed sounded bitter when he spoke. "Our country got itself into a world of trouble by being in debt. Lots of people saw this coming, but nobody really knew what to do about it. We kept borrowing more and more, and things like plummeting stocks and housing, lack of energy resources and declining credit all made this mess we're in now."

Frank was indignant. "You mean to tell me that because we owe a bunch of foreigners some money that means we ran out of food and fuel? Why don't we just send our troops in and take care of the problem?"

Marty sighed. "Frank, I know it's difficult, but the reasons we are in this mess are not really anything we can change at this point. The whole world is in a big mess. However, we do have some pressing problems that need to be addressed first. I'll stop by your house tomorrow afternoon and we can talk privately about this, okay?"

"Fine. But I still think we need to remember what made this country great and get ourselves back on our feet again."

"You are absolutely right," Marty agreed. "But first we need to figure out how we're going to survive the coming months and years."

A deep silence descended on the crowd as Hope absorbed Marty's words. Some small part of her had held onto the hope that maybe things would get better and go back to the way they were, but as time passed that hope was fading. *This time of year we're usually getting ready for the holidays… I don't think Santa's going to be able to help us now.*

Clearing his throat, Marty continued. "My concern is that there has already been one security breach in the neighborhood. One of the men that we have watching our eastern front entry point allowed persons of unknown origins to cross into our area."

"Foreigners?" Frank yelled.

"No, not foreigners exactly, just people from other areas that were actually looking to rob some of the homes here. They were apprehended during a routine patrol I was on with Ed."

"That whole thing was ridiculous," Sharon sputtered. "What do these people think they're doing, anyway? Nobody has any electricity across the whole country. What good does it do to steal televisions and computers when they can't be used?"

"Most of us have no idea how long this will last," Marty answered quietly. "Looting and robbing is kind of like saving for a rainy day. People are banking on the fact that at some point in the future everything will get back to normal."

"Did ya shoot 'em?" Frank asked. "Cause if ya didn't, then that's too bad. They shoulda been shot."

Marty was clearly trying to suppress a grin. "No, sir, we did not shoot anyone. We simply escorted them out, but we did let them know that an execution was a definite possibility. Hopefully that will stop them from coming back."

"Probably not. Besides, there'll be more," Hope said quietly.

Marty looked at her and nodded. "There will be more."

Corinne, quiet until this point, asked, "Marty, what are you proposing we do now? Get more security? I don't see how that will be possible since we have a number of neighbors that won't even participate in meetings like this one."

"You're right, Corinne. There's a small contingent in this area trying to establish that they are in charge and have begun holding secret meetings to discuss a sort of takeover."

"Hmmph. Can't be too secret if you're tellin' us about it," Frank noted.

"I have sources they are unaware of. But to answer your question, Corinne, no, I don't think more security is the answer. I see us as having problems on several levels. First and most obvious is the security. As people become more desperate I'm afraid a perimeter breach will mean folks will be in here not just stealing our stuff but maybe even worse. I don't like the idea of fending off violent intruders. But more importantly, we're all aware that we have limited food and water resources. Water is a big problem. We've got rain barrels, but that hasn't yielded much. The creek on the west side of the neighborhood has come in handy for a water source, but we haven't had much rain in the past couple of weeks. If that creek dries up we'll be —"

"Up a creek," Hope finished. "Obviously we can't last long without water, but it's not like we can just lock our houses up and leave."

"That's exactly what we may have to do. I would like to propose that we move everyone to a safer location. My sources say that there is a community further north, up in the Middlesex area, where folks have plenty of food and water and have created a sustainable village. They've actually been living there since before the collapse."

"Sustainable village?" Doubt was evident in Ed's voice. "What, exactly, does that mean?"

"It means they're living in a rural environment and have a greater ability to fend for themselves. There's more room to grow food and less people to cause trouble. The creek that starts in our neighborhood ends up feeding into the river that runs alongside Middlesex, so they have a better water source. Security is tight and I don't think they'll be letting strangers in for much longer. I'd like to propose that we organize ourselves and get on over there before things get much worse here."

"Why will it be better there? I'm not sure we should leave what we know," Ed said.

"It will be better because this is a group that has been living off the grid for some time now. They're used to not depending on outside resources for things like food and water. I've heard a doctor lives there, and that means some form of health care. Plus, they've been an established community for a while."

"No power struggles," Hope said, thinking of the small contingent of people in her neighborhood looking to take over.

"No power struggles," Marty agreed.

"But how are we going to get there when we don't have any gas for the cars?" Joan asked.

"We'll do it the old fashioned way, missy. We'll use our God-given two legs and walk." Frank's tone clearly indicated his disgust.

"That's exactly what we'll do," Marty added. "In fact, I have a plan."

"Wait a minute," Joan interrupted. "Do you mean you want us to leave our homes behind and go live out in the middle of nowhere? You've got to be kidding me. What's going to happen to our houses?"

"What's going to happen to us if we don't?" Hope asked. Leaving her home behind was terrifying on several levels, but Marty was right. They couldn't survive without water. "I can see the truth of what you're saying, Marty, but some may be a little hesitant to leave."

"I'm not forcing anyone to do anything. All I'm saying is it might be a better option for us to get to safer ground. I, for one, am planning on heading out there. If anyone wants to join me, I'll see to it we get there safely. For those of us who choose to go up to Middlesex, well, I can only guess that somehow word will get out to others where we went," Marty answered, looking directly at Hope.

"And you really think we'll be better off up there?"

Marty nodded. "Not a doubt in my mind. Our society has disintegrated, and we're rapidly running out of resources. We need to get to a safe haven. Unfortunately, our little suburban paradise here isn't enough."

Throughout the rest of the evening the neighbors debated and argued the merits of moving. Opinions were strong on both sides, but by the end of the night most people had made some sort of decision for themselves.

As neighbors prepared to leave in groups to go back to their houses, Marty approached Hope. "Well? Staying or going?"

She hesitated briefly. "There's not much choice, is there?" she asked softly. "My first priority is my kids. I need to do everything I can to keep them safe and provide for them. And you're right, you know. Another summer like we had this year and that creek will be bone dry. I thought there'd be more rain this fall, but... We'll go with you."

"It's a good move, Hope. You'll be safer with us."

Hope wanted to believe him, but the week that followed found doubt crowding her heart and mind. What if it was riskier to travel on the roads to another town? What if the sustainable village Marty spoke of refused to take them in? But most importantly, what if Harlan came back and they were gone?

Chapter 3

Two nights after the dinner meeting Hope opened her eyes to complete darkness. *Must be about three in the morning,* she thought. *Why am I awake?*

A moment later she heard it. Guttural shrieks, screams... She shivered, rubbing her arms where goose bumps were raised. *What the hell is that?* Grabbing a baseball bat from the corner by her bed, she crept to her window and peeked outside. She couldn't see anything, but the howls had stopped. Coyote? Could they be that close that she could hear them through a closed window?

Moments later she saw them, dark figures running down the street. People running away. She sank down from the window even though she knew they couldn't see her. *What the hell?* Who were they, and where did they come from?

She crawled into the living room, afraid to stand in case anyone was outside the house. She didn't want to be seen.

Sitting on the floor, she leaned her back against the front door and waited for dawn. She was ready to defend her children with whatever she had. *They'll have to get through me, first.*

*****

The next day Marty stopped by to tell her that another home on her street had been broken into. Her neighbors, a twenty-something formerly professional couple, were badly beaten and left for dead. The shrieks that she'd heard the night before echoed through her mind. For whatever reason, guards had not been positioned at the entry points to the neighborhood. *We need more protection. Dear God, what if…*

The thought was too unbearable to finish. Her decision to leave was clearly the right one. They couldn't go on like this.

As she sorted through their clothes, deciding what to bring and what to leave behind, Hope thought about what might happen if others came looking to raid the homes in the neighborhood. *Upper middle class suburbia just isn't what it used to be*, she thought wryly, placing a sweater on top of the pile of clothes that would be carried with them.

Around twenty-five people decided to make the journey to Middlesex. Each person was assigned to carry a backpack, while wagons, carriages, and strollers were gathered to carry supplies.

"Mommy, how long will it take us to get there?"

Hope paused, welcoming the break her daughter offered. "This is just a guess, but I think it might take us five or six days."

Sandy looked horrified. "We're going to walk for five or six days? Why will it take us so long?" Her face brightened for a moment. "I know, maybe we can run and get there quicker."

Hope smiled. "The place we're going to is about thirty five miles from our house. But remember, we can only go as fast as the slowest person that is with us. We have to stay together as a group, and some people don't have the same amount of energy you have."

Sandy's forehead wrinkled. "So, what you mean is we can only walk as fast as Mrs. Fletcher."

"That's right. We don't want to leave her behind, do we?"

"No, I guess not. But mommy, are you sure daddy will know where to find us? What if he can't find us?"

"It doesn't really matter, Sandy, I've already told you he's not coming back." Jared stood in the doorway, arms crossed in a defensive position.

"Jared, please don't speak to your sister like that. We don't know where your father is, and we don't know what happened to him. For now, let's hope for the best and assume he's doing everything he can to get back. To answer your question, Sandy, your father will know where to find us because I'm leaving messages for him if he comes back. Don't worry; he'll know exactly where we went."

"So, we're like supposed to walk for a week and get to some strange place full of people we don't know who might or might not take us in and then hope that Dad can walk to us after he's been wherever he's been?" Jared snorted. "Right, Mom. That'll work."

Hope stepped in front of Jared. "Now you listen to me, young man. I understand how you're feeling. I'm just as upset as you are about this. But right now we've got each other, and we've got to try to survive as best we can. We're leaving in two days, and I know if your father were here he would tell me it's the right thing to do. Now you'd better figure out a way to change your attitude, and you'd better figure it out quick."

"Or what? You'll take my video games away?" Jared turned and stalked down the hall to his room.

"No, Jared, or you won't be able to hold your heart open." It didn't matter if Jared heard her or not, she knew he wasn't ready to understand what she was saying. Every day that went by broke her heart a little bit more as she watched her children struggle, and she could clearly see their last hope for a better life right now was to go somewhere else. *Thank god for Marty*, she thought, not for the first time that week. If anyone could get them to safety, she knew Marty could do it. At least, that's what they were all counting on.

Marty's plan for moving everyone was simple. Two days after the break-in at her neighbors they gathered at the Warren's house again, this time ready to move.

"Okay, I need to form a rectangle," Marty called out. "I need all the young, strong men and women on the outside, and children and older folks on the inside. My outside rectangle will receive weapons. You are our line of defense in case of an attack from any of the rogue wackos wandering the streets. I will be at the rear of the formation and will give the order to shoot if necessary. Aim for the heart. If you have to shoot, shoot to kill."

As everybody gathered and formed an orderly rectangle formation, Hope's heart leapt into her throat. Her son, Jared, had placed himself on the outside of the formation.

"Jared, honey, why don't you –"

"No, Mom, I'm part of the first line of defense. I'm young and strong and I know how to shoot." Jared held his head high, and added, "It's what Dad would have wanted."

Hope's heart shattered as memories of Jared, with his newborn head full of peach fuzz, flashed through her mind. He was a part of her, and yet she needed to let him do this. Unable to speak, she simply nodded. Hope took a position on the outside as well, three people behind Jared. *God help the person who tries to hurt my son*, she thought. *I will tear a hole in his throat.*

And so the long walk began, one step at a time. Initially people talked and joked, but as the day wore on and blisters started to form on hands and feet the mood became more somber. There were many stops for bathroom breaks, and the children's complaints grew as the hours dragged by. Ruth and Frank, the most elderly of the group, threw constant apologies out to everyone.

"We are so sorry to hold you all up. If you want to go ahead we'll be okay," Ruth said, shaking her head. "I know I'm the slowest here, and I don't want to be the reason it takes so long."

Murmurs of disagreement rippled through the group. "We're not leaving you behind, Ruth," people told her.

"You can't get rid of us that easily," Ed joked, trying to make light of the situation.

At dusk they stopped, having crossed the bridge and traveled almost seven miles for the day. "We can make our camp behind that strip mall over there," Marty announced, pointing to a deserted area. "After we set the tents up we can eat, then everyone goes to sleep. We need our rest, we've got a long ways to go still. We'll take turns guarding the area, and try to be up at first light to keep moving."

With everyone working together, pitching tents went quickly. A large fire was built and a feast of squirrel and rabbit, courtesy of Marty and Ed, was enjoyed for dinner. "Make sure the fire gets put out quickly," Marty told them. "I don't want that light on any longer than it has to be."

"But it might be nice to sit around a campfire together," Joan complained.

"And it might be nice if we stayed hidden from anyone who might be out there," Marty retorted. With a sniff, Joan hustled her kids into their tent for the evening. Hope was again glad that Marty was in charge. *He's right, we can't take chances.*

Hope was surprised at how tired she was and more than a little grateful that sleep came quickly. Jared and Sandy, thankfully, fell asleep just as soon as they settled into the tent. The one heavy blanket Hope had carried with them served to keep the family warm, and they used sweatshirts as makeshift pillows.

It seemed like only minutes later that Hope was awake, startled out of her sleep. Disoriented in the murky darkness, she lay still, wondering what was out there. Slowly it occurred to her there was a rhythmic tapping on the tent. Sometime during the night a steady rain had begun, making the early dawn hours gray and darker than normal.

I do miss the weather channel, even if they got it wrong most of the time, Hope thought. *Put that on my list of things I used to take for granted.*

The group of campers was slow to rise, as nobody was looking forward to the long, wet walk they faced.

"C'mon, folks, the sooner we get moving the sooner we get to our destination," Marty urged everyone. "We'll be okay, just put one foot in front of another and keep moving. Don't think, just move. Let's go."

After sharing a meager breakfast of potatoes and bitter chicory coffee the group got back on the road. The rain made talk a little more difficult, but there were some who tried to keep everyone's spirits up with their banter.

"I've been meaning to start training for a marathon," Ed joked. "I just didn't know I'd be doing it so soon."

"Hey, Ed, at the rate you can run you'll be training for the Lead Man competition instead of the Iron Man."

"Oh yeah? Maybe we should have a little jousting competition at our next campsite."

The attack happened so quickly there was barely time to react. From behind a storefront on the right a group of strangers lunged at them, faces masked with grime and desperation. Looking into the frenzied eyes of a bearded man as he rushed toward her, Hope knew that these were people that had lost their grip on sanity. Raising her gun she fired off a shot in conjunction with Marty's booming command.

"Fire!"

Chapter 4

Gunshots mingled with screams. Hope took aim and fired, but her attacker kept coming. She took a step backward, but he was on her, pulling her toward him. Her breath came in short gasps as she kicked and punched, clawing at his face. Grabbing her, he pulled her onto the ground as she struggled against him. Punching and kicking did no good as his weight bore down on her, pinning her to the ground. He raised a knife, and without thinking she tried to roll to her side, struggling to dislodge the man from her body before he killed her. As his arm went back he suddenly fell off of her. Breathing heavily, Hope watched as Marty threw the man to the ground and kicked him in the stomach. Taking aim, Marty prepared to shoot the attacker, but was momentarily distracted by a ghastly scream coming from their group.

One of the neighbors from their group, Hilary, was being dragged off by two men. As she struggled and screamed, one of the crazies, as Hope now thought of them, grabbed Hilary's hair, pulled her head back and kicked her in the gut. Her screams stopped, but they used her as a shield so Marty and the others couldn't shoot. Just as quickly as they'd arrived they were gone, taking Hilary with them.

Hope struggled for her own breath as she watched her neighbor's body being dragged off to a probable death. Crawling to Jared and Sandy, Hope gathered her children into her arms and held them tight.

The sound of sobbing broke out after a moment of silence. Jeff, Hilary's husband, sat on the ground holding his head in his hands. Friends gathered around him.

"Is anyone injured?" Marty asked in a subdued voice. "Ruth, Frank, are you okay?"

Ruth and Frank nodded, silent. Hope sat, stunned and uncertain of what to say to Jeff. He and Hilary had only been married for two years. As successful twenty-somethings, they had their whole lives ahead of them and had planned on living the American dream of children and a dog in suburbia. They had no children and their dog was long gone. The dream had become a nightmare.

"I don't mean to sound harsh, but I think the best thing is for us to get up and keep moving." Marty's voice sounded shaky. "We don't know who those people were or if there are more of them, and I really don't ever want to see them again. They may be off somewhere re-grouping, and I wouldn't be surprised if they plan on coming back."

Jeff looked up at Marty. "But, we can't just let them take her."

Marty hesitated for a moment. "I'm sorry, man, I really am. But I think that for our safety we need to get out of here. I counted more than fifty people in that group, and who knows how many more they have back at their camp. I want to get her, but I'm afraid we're outnumbered. And it looks like they took a lot of our supplies. I'm sorry, Jeff, I really am…" His voice trailed off as he stood, obviously uncomfortable and holding his right arm.

"Marty, are you hurt?" Hope asked. "It looks like you're bleeding."

Marty nodded. "Yeah, my arm got cut. I'm okay, though, it's not a bad wound. I'll wrap it as we keep walking. But we really need to keep walking."

Shaken and wary, the group somehow managed to pick up the few things left on the ground and get moving again. By unspoken consent Jeff was put in the middle of the group, as if they could form a barrier of support that might somehow help him.

Trudging through the muddy street, soaked by the steady rain, adrenaline coursed through Hope. She glanced around nervously, hoping there wouldn't be another attack, knowing in her heart this little group could not withstand any more violence that day. Shivering, Hope put her arms around her children as they pushed on, grateful once again that they had been spared.

Marty hid his pain well. He had already soaked two shirts with his blood, with no signs of slowing down.

"Marty, please, let's take cover somewhere so I can wrap your arm properly. We can't afford to have something happen to you now," Hope pleaded with him. *We'll die.* Her unspoken thought hung in the air.

Marty agreed. "I hate stopping, but you're right. Let's find a place to stop."

"Right here is good." Hope had been so focused on Marty that the strange voice caused her to jump. Jared drew his weapon, aiming at the heart of the stranger before them.

"You might want to put that away, son, seeing as how I'm armed too. No point in us both killing each other." The stranger was tall and lean, with several days growth of a beard and shaggy dark hair that reached just below his collar. His direct gaze fell on Marty. "It looks like you folks have seen some trouble."

There was a brief silence before Marty spoke. "We were attacked just a little ways back. Out of nowhere a group of—" Marty struggled to spit out the words, "people came at us. They took one of our group, grabbed her by the hair and took off with her and a bunch of our supplies."

The stranger nodded. "We've been seeing them around here. You're lucky they just took her, it could've been worse. They've done a fair bit of killing, but then again, so have we." He looked the group over and sighed. "You'd better come with me. I assume you're heading out to the farms, right?"

"I don't think that's any of your business," Jared told him defiantly. "Besides, why should we go with you?"

The stranger nodded. "I'm glad to see you've still got some spunk left in you." The smile faded as he added, "What you just went through could have affected you in a whole different way."

"What do you mean, the farms?" Hope asked.

"It's what some folks are calling the village. I call it the farms because several working farms are back there. I've seen a few groups of people heading through here, trying to get up to the farms and find safety."

"Tell us the truth. Is it safe out there?" Sharon asked in a tentative voice.

The stranger nodded. "It's safer than most places. Plus, there's plenty of food and water for an entire village. My wife and I, we've been trying to help folks get through here safely. There's a whole group of people, they're just plain crazy. I don't know where they came from, but you've seen what they can do. We try to act as a sort of safe haven to help you get where you need to go."

"Like a stop on the underground railroad," Sandy piped in.

For the first time, the stranger smiled. "Exactly. Like a stop on the underground railroad. If you follow me I'll take you back to our house. My wife can help you with that wound," he nodded at Marty, "and you can rest a while. You'll be safe with us, and I can draw you a map with a better route to the farms."

Seconds ticked by as the rain drizzled down. Hope held her breath and looked to Marty. After a moment he gave a brief nod, indicating they should follow the stranger.

It took them almost fifteen minutes to trek to the man's house. During this time they learned his name was Ellis and his wife's name was Shawna. Ellis told the group of the many people that had come through and of his struggles to help them. "Shawna and I, we see it as our responsibility to make this a better place. Once everything collapsed we figured it would get bad, and we were right. We've been stockpiling supplies for years now, waiting for this to happen."

Hope and Marty exchanged a glance. They had heard of people like this, people who were prepared for the eventuality of a complete economic and social collapse. For the first time ever, Hope was thankful they existed.

"You can all spend the night in the house. We'll spread you out in the bedrooms and living room, or wherever there's space. Shawna is probably cooking right now since I told her I was going out on patrol to see if there were any stragglers." He glanced over at Marty. "That's what I call folks who come through here looking for a better place, stragglers. Everyone seems to sort of stumble their way in."

Soon they were at Ellis's home, a two story white clapboard farmhouse beginning to show signs of weathering. A wraparound porch held several rockers, and a cloud of smoke rose from the chimney.

Hope felt like she had come home.

Ellis ushered everyone inside and introductions were made all around. His wife, Shawna, seemed pleased to meet them. "I'm glad Ellis found you," she told Hope quietly. "It's terrible what's happening out there, and we've been trying to help any way we can."

"Shawna made enough food for everyone," Ellis announced. "In the meantime, feel free to use the bathrooms and get cleaned up."

There was a moment of stunned silence before anyone spoke. "Bathrooms?" Jared squeaked. "But how…"

Ellis smiled at the boy. "Out here we've got well water and what you might call alternative energy. Shawna and I have lived off the grid for quite a while now. We didn't want to rely on the big energy companies for anything."

"What do you mean, off the grid?" Joan asked, her face wrinkled in confusion.

"It means we don't have heating and electricity the way most people do," Shawna explained. "We have a combination of solar, wind and bio-energy sources that provide us with everything we need."

"You mean you have running water?" Ed asked, incredulous.

"Yes, as well as heat and hot water." Pride was evident in Ellis's voice.

Tears welled up in Hope's eyes, and she had to blink them away. "I think our first order of business is to get Marty cleaned up. He's still bleeding."

Shawna reached out to touch Marty's arm. "Come with me and I'll take care of that. I have a stockpile of medicinal supplies that we can use."

Of course they have medicinal supplies, Hope thought, wondering if she was on the verge of hysteria. *Why wouldn't they?*

"Mom," Jared interrupted Hope's thoughts. "Are you okay? You look kind of weird."

"I'll be fine," Hope reassured him. "I'm overwhelmed, that's all. I feel like we've won the lottery."

"Your timing is perfect," Ellis said, coming into the room. "Do you know what today is?"

"Our lucky day?" Sandy said.

Ellis smiled. "I think it's a lucky day for all of us, because we get to celebrate Thanksgiving together. We have a lot to be thankful for, don't you think?"

"Today is Thanksgiving?" Sandy's eyes were huge.

How had she forgotten the date? And were they lucky? Hope's first thought was No, life sucks, but she knew he was right. Her kids were safe and they were with her. Her husband was gone, but maybe he had reasons for not coming back. She had no control over him.

Maybe she was better off without him, anyway. Maybe this new world gave them all a chance to start over. After all, the pioneers that came to this country had survived—flourished, even. She would too.

Later that day, with the twenty-four of them welcomed into the farmhouse, they gathered throughout the rooms for dinner. Some sat at the dining room table, others in the kitchen, living room and family room. Venison and fresh vegetables were passed around, and for the first time in months Hope's edge of anxiety eased.

After dinner, the core group gathered in the kitchen to discuss their next step.

"I'm going to draw you a map," Ellis told Marty. "If you follow this trail you'll be much safer. There are others along the way who will look out for you, too. You may not see them but you'll be much better protected than you would be on the main road."

Marty shook his head. "To be honest with you, I wasn't sure what would be better, but I thought that traveling the main road would be safer than hiking through the woods."

Ellis nodded. "I know, it's not an easy call to make. But around here the lunatics that attacked you seem to hang around the main route. I think they may be hiding out in empty storefronts."

"How will we know when we get there?" Sandy asked. "Is there a sign?"

Shawna gave the little girl a hug. "Don't worry, honey, I promise you'll know when you get there. I don't think you've ever seen anything like this before."

Again, Hope's eyes filled with tears. "Thank you. I don't know what else to say, except thank you."

"You're welcome."

Chapter 5

The following day dawned crisp and clear. "I hate walking through the rain," Jared muttered, looking out the window. "I hope this weather lasts at least until we get there."

Setting off on their journey again, Hope and Marty paused in front of the farmhouse. "I know we've all said it already, but thanks. Your kindness will be remembered," Marty told the couple.

"It's what we do," Shawna replied. "Just take care of yourself, and remember to take the rest of those pills I gave you to keep an infection from getting into your arm. I wish you could stay, but we don't have the room. You'll find plenty of space for you at the village."

"I think we need to go now," Joan interrupted. "We've got a long walk, and I am not looking forward to tics and mosquitoes."

Hope and Marty looked at each other, trying not to laugh. Joan seemed to have been able to find plenty to complain about, and for some reason both Hope and Marty had started to find it amusing.

"What's so funny?" Joan demanded.

"Nothing, you're right, let's get going," Marty said, obviously struggling to keep a straight face. He turned back to Ellis. "Are you sure it's okay to leave Jeff with you?"

Ellis nodded. "I think it's best. He's not doing so well, and who can blame him after what he saw happen to his wife. Everyone handles things differently, and we'll make sure he has a quiet place to rest for a while and try to pull himself together. If he decides to join you, I'll see to it that he gets there."

There wasn't much choice, Hope realized as she listened to the exchange. Jeff had lapsed into silence, unable and unwilling to communicate with anyone after Hilary was dragged off to a horrible fate. For the most part he sat and stared into space, lost in a world of his own. She hoped that he would someday be able to accept that there wasn't anything they could do, but for now he needed to rest.

With waves and a few more hugs, the group set off. Looking at the map, Marty announced, "I think this route may actually be a little bit shorter. Hopefully we'll be there in a few days."

The next three days followed the same routine. Rising at dawn, they ate breakfast and set off on the designated path. When the sun was high overhead they stopped for a quick lunch, and set off again until dusk. The night camps were quickly set up while dinner was prepared. Ellis and Shawna had given the group a supply of extra food and water, making meals more enjoyable and less worrisome.

Occasionally Hope glanced at the woods around her, feeling a stir at the back of her neck as if she were being watched. "I feel it too," Marty told her on the second day. "Just keep moving. Ellis said others are watching out for us. If they mean us harm they'll make themselves known."

But they had no more incidents like the one they had on the main road. Toward the end of the third day the group struggled up a steep hill, carrying an exhausted Ruth and assisting Frank through the terrain. The clearing at the top allowed them to see for miles.

Silence filled the air as the group took in the sight before them. Finally, Jared asked in a cracked voice, "What is that?"

"I believe that is the village," Marty answered quietly.

"I know, but what am I looking at?"

In the valley below sat a cluster of twelve homes, some with smoke rising from the chimneys. Hope counted three barns and what looked like several more storage sheds. Horses and cows were in the fields farthest from the homes.

"It looks like they've built a wall," Hope told her son. "They must have gathered anything they could and built a wall to keep everyone safe."

It was a bizarre combination of objects that circled the tiny village, including hand piled stones, fencing materials, sandbags and what looked to be piles of old furniture.

"I'll bet it's very safe in there," Sharon added.

"Is that where we're going to live?" Sandy asked.

"That's the place," Jared said. "Looks like we'll be okay in there."

"Is that where we're going to have Christmas?" Sandy said.

"How can you be thinking about Christmas?" Jared said.

"How could I not?" Sandy countered. "We just had Thanksgiving, and everyone knows Christmas is next."

Hope laughed. "Yes, that is where we're going to have Christmas."

"It won't be the same," Marty said. "But it will be good. We'll make it good."

"We're together, so it will be wonderful. It will just be a different kind of Christmas," Hope said. "Now let's go see if we can find a way into our new home."

Christmas Miracles

Gloria J. Savage-Early

For my many family members and friends, especially my parents and grandparents, Thomas Leon Savage, Sr., Beatrice Walton Savage, Daniel Savage, Annie Peele Savage, James Edward Walton, and Matilda Stewart Walton. Most of all I dedicate this story and my very life to Jesus Christ.

Chapter 1

Thoughts of childhood Christmases brought warm feelings as Dominique Cornelia Peele reflected on her years of celebrating with family members and friends. *Good heavens, who doesn't get thrilled about Christmas? Christmas is so exciting with all the lights, gifts, food, music, and get-togethers. It's always so enjoyable to reflect on all the exciting things that have happened over the many years of celebrating Christmas in even one family.*

She was from a large family of seven children, and she was the sixth child. She was often being told what to do by her older siblings. Even her younger sibling, because he was a male child, wanted to tell her what to do at time. But Dominique didn't mind because she had no desire to be in charge. She was not a "spotlight" kind of person, and she saw his actions as him being a protective brother.

Dominique was often quiet, but her brain was always working. She seldom had much to say because she was attentively listening to everything around her. She had a special way of showing care and concern for people and she never wanted people mistreated, not even the ones who mistreated her or the ones who mistreated others.

Dominique's Aunt Leta had plans for the Christmas of 2014. She was planning a family dinner the first three Saturdays of

December at 4:00 p.m. culminating with a big family dinner on Christmas Eve at 2:00 p.m. Four family members would each host one of the three Saturday dinners, and Aunt Leta would host the big Christmas Eve dinner. She had let everyone know that they could miss one of the three Saturday dinners but everyone was expected to attend the big Christmas Eve dinner.

"You can miss only one of the first three dinners," said Aunt Leta after church one Sunday. "But don't forget, I expect everyone to attend the big dinner at my house. And I expect everyone to be on time," she continued with a very serious look on her face.

Dominique could visualize Aunt Leta at church, full of excitement about the plans for the Christmas dinners. Everyone knew how Aunt Leta could be with such things – straightforward. Everyone also knew that Aunt Leta was an exceptional cook. She had a reputation for putting several pounds on a great number of people up and down the East Coast, especially in the states of Virginia and North Carolina.

"I might miss two of the Saturday dinners," whispered Dominique to Cousin Oveta, "but I will not miss Christmas Eve dinner at Aunt Leta's house. That is for sure."

They laughed together as they carried on about the traditional Christmas dinners passed down through generations in the Peele Family. Those dinners were something to get excited about because they were always carried out in an excellent manner and the food was plentiful and delicious. What more could anyone want at Christmastime, except maybe a few presents? At those big family dinners family members would talk about Christmas traditions and miracles and reflect on their favorite and most exciting Christmases. Everybody had a grand time. Everybody laughed and cried, and the great part was that sometimes the tears were simply a result of laughing so hard that tears flowed from overwhelming joy.

Traditions were added each year as the family grew, and new families added their own little customs. Hearing about a so-called new tradition from a newlywed couple was exciting. Usually that tradition turned out to be just a spin on an old family tradition. For example, Cousin Grace was thrilled to announce several years ago that she was wearing red every day in December and calling a different family member each day in December.

"Both of those have been in this family for years," announced Aunt Leta four Christmases ago.

Cousin Grace even had her husband, Justin, wearing something red to the family Christmas events. He didn't seem to mind, and family members often remarked on how attractive they looked.

"I don't ever see anyone wear red the entire month," Grace said one year.

"And you live where? California," said Aunt Leta. "You are not here in the area Grace, which is why you don't see a lot of the traditions being carried out. Come home more often."

Everyone laughed so hard that year because different family members were always trying to come up with something new and innovative. Grace had moved to California with her husband and did not come home as regularly as she used to. She was definitely out of the loop.

"Yeah Cousin Grace," said Johnathan, Dominique's youngest brother. "You might need to come home just a little more often."

"Grace, you have to get up early in the morning to pull one on Aunt Leta," said Dominique. "She knows just about everything that goes on in the Peele family."

"She knows about what goes on in a few other families too," added Johnathan with a hearty laugh.

Everyone laughed at him, when Aunt Leta said, "I cannot help it if people like to tell me what is going on in their families. I am happy to listen, but some people just get bothered because I don't share those goings-on with them."

"Ooh," said Dominique.

"She's right," said Johnathan, no longer laughing. "No shame in my game. Yes, I tried to get some information from Aunt Leta and didn't get a thing."

Aunt Leta knew Johnathan wanted information about all the attractive young ladies in the neighborhood. She was determined not to give him information about her "neighborhood girls." If he wanted to know about them he would have to get to know them on his own terms.

Chapter 2

The thirty-one days in December were simply not enough for the Peele family to celebrate Christmas, so they generally celebrated all year long in at least some small way. Her father John Michael Peele was called Michael because his father, John Edward Peele, was called John. Sometimes they used middle names to eliminate confusion, which often caused more confusion. Michael was twenty-three years old when he married Dominique's mother, Beatrice "Bea" Walton, who was only nineteen at the time of their marriage. They were two happy youngsters.

Michael was from Mathews, Virginia and he met Bea in Hampton, Virginia. He was working as a welder at the Newport News Shipyard, which built nuclear-powered aircraft carriers and submarines for the Navy. Michael went through the shipyard's apprentice school to learn his trade. The school paid him for a forty-hour week, which included classroom time. He started at the shipyard right out of high school and had been working there five years when he married Bea. Bea, still living in Gloucester County, was a student at Thomas Nelson Community College studying to become a Registered Nurse. She loved helping people and wanted to be in the medical field. She lived in Hayes, the southern part of the county, so Thomas Nelson was closer to where she lived than Rappahannock Community College, which was in northern Gloucester. She didn't mind the drive over the Coleman Bridge, which crossed the York River, even though she was late a few times due to unscheduled bridge openings.

Michael and Bea met on a rainy night at Bethel High School, where a basketball game was being played between TNCC and the College of Southern Maryland from La Plata. Michael was with his younger brother Gregory, who was dating Bea's friend and nursing classmate, Anita. Bea and Anita were busy with a school project so Bea gave Anita a ride to the game.

"The rain is pouring," said Anita as she and Bea entered the building crammed under a small umbrella.

"Hello ladies, come on in," said Gregory as he held the door for Anita and Bea.

"I figured you would beat us here," said Anita. "We were trying hard to finish a project. Gregory, do you remember my friend Bea?"

"Sure, I do. How are you this rainy night?"

"I am fine. How are you Gregory?"

"A little dryer than the two of you, I think. It wasn't raining as hard when we arrived. Glad we made it in before the downpour."

"We? Who's with you?" Anita asked.

"Michael rode along with me to watch the game. You ladies haven't missed much."

"Are we winning?" Bea asked.

"It's a little back and forth right now," said Gregory. "Those Maryland guys are tough. They're gonna be hard to beat. Their guard is as quick as lightning, and he's already stealing passes."

"I'm too tired to stay and watch them get beat," said Bea.

"Oh, come on Bea, stay for a little while," said Anita. "Maybe the rain will let up. Come on." Anita locked her arm into Bea's and pulled her along.

"No," said Bea. "I'm tired."

"Come on, you can keep my brother company," said Michael.

Bea stopped and looked at Anita. "I hope you're trying to fix me up with anyone," said Bea in a low voice.

"I didn't know he was coming," Anita whispered. "I was just expecting Gregory."

They enter the gymnasium and Michael stood and waved.

"I guess you didn't like the seats I picked," said Gregory.

"They were okay, I just thought these were a little better," said Michael. "At least the ladies didn't have to walk the entire length of the gym floor."

"Hey Michael," said Anita. "This is my friend Bea from school."

"I'm pleased to meet you Bea, said Michael. "How are you tonight?"

"A bit tired," said Bea. "Pleased to meet you as well."

Michael stood and shook Bea's hand, and then the four sat down to watch the game. The score continued to go back and forth with Southern Maryland slightly in the lead after each turnover. Bea did not want to see TNCC loose, but she was glad she stayed. She welcomed a different scenario. Besides, Gregory was very attractive and had a very pleasant temperament. The two hit it off well and became quite the couple. And as they say, *the rest was history.*

Chapter 3

Just fourteen months after Michael and Bea were married Frances Elizabeth, their first-born, was born into their family of two. Michael was twenty-four and Bea was only twenty when she arrived in 1972. They were happy and excited but a new baby certainly put a strain on their young marriage. Michael began to work overtime to increase their income, while Bea was busy slowly progressing through school and often feeling too tired to complete her homework. She was required to take two sequential biology classes in anatomy and physiology. She would fall asleep studying the structure and functions of cells, tissues, and systems of the human body. Bea did not know the human body was so complex until she was studying nursing. Sometimes Michael would hear Bea talking in her sleep about subjects she was studying.

"A cell is the smallest unit of life," said Bea as if she was studying for some sort of test. "A tissue is a group of similar cells that perform a common function. An organ is…." She would stop so tired she could not say another word.

"You're studying in your sleep again honey," said Michael, tired himself and wanting to get some sleep.

Neither of them could wait for the weekend so they could to get some much-needed rest. Sometimes a friend or relative would keep Frances Elizabeth on Saturday just so they could get some rest. They were very committed to their work and studies and their new "bundle of joy" brought them so much enjoyment, but she also made their lives very challenging. Their bodies were young yet they could only take so much.

*****

Michael and Bea worked through the challenges of their busy lives, and Bea finally completed her Associates Degree in Nursing. A two-year degree had taken her almost four years to complete. Starting a family early had caused her to slow her pace, but she was happy to finally graduate.

Bea cooked Michael a very special candlelight dinner one night in the middle of the week. Busy with school and Frances Elizabeth, she had not taken time for some of the simple pleasures of life. Michael was thrilled to sit down with Bea and enjoy a nice meal with soft background music and good conversation. Frances Elizabeth was with a sitter and it was just the two of them.

"I suppose we should be thinking about a playmate for Frances Elizabeth now that I've finished school," said Bea.

"What do you mean by playmate," said Michael.

"Another child," said Bea. "Frances Elizabeth is almost two and a half."

"Yes, but I thought you wanted to continue college and get you bachelor's degree in nursing."

"I do, but…"

"But what?" Michael interrupted.

The shortness in Michael voice caused Bea some hesitation. She was not sure what to say next, so there was quietness at the table, which seemed to put a damper on the mood of the evening.

"Would you like some dessert?" she asked changing the subject.

"Sure, why not," said Michael.

Bea brought in the dessert and they sat quietly as they continued the meal. It appeared that neither of them saved room for dessert. The silence was killing Bea. She just didn't know what to say so she kept quiet. Finally, Michael broke the ice.

"Bea," he said. "I just thought maybe we could take some time for a vacation. Just the two of us. We've been pushing so hard since we got married. I think we need a break. I know I do."

"I just thought," said Bea. Then she stopped and began to cry.

"What?" Michael said. "Are you excited about the vacation or are you thinking that we can't afford it?"

"I'm pregnant," said Bea.

She blurted it out without looking at Michael for fear that he might be disappointed. Silence filled the room once again. She put her face in her hands and continued to cry.

"Wow," said Michael. "I didn't see that one coming. Are you sure you're pregnant?" Michael said the word pregnant slowly, as if he had difficulty getting it out of his mouth.

"The doctor seems sure," Bea finally said as she looked into Michael's eyes.

"How are you going to work?" Michael said.

"Women do it everyday."

"What about Frances Elizabeth?"

"What about her?"

"Who will take care of her?"

"She'll have to go to a sitter. Just like she did when I was in school."

"What about when the new baby comes?"

"Will you listen to yourself? What are you talking about? People have children every day and they work it out."

"I am not ready for this."

"Well, you better get ready."

Bea's whole demeanor had changed since the start of dinner. She got up and began to clear the table. She was even sadder now. *The beautiful dinner has been ruined.* Michael prepared for bed while Bea cleared the table and washed the dishes. The quiet continued into the night. Not another word was said for the rest of the night.

Chapter 4

Michael Edward Peele was born in January of 1975. They decided to call him Edward for much the same reason his father was called Michael, which was his middle name. Michael was happy to have a son. What seemed like disappointment months ago was now "showers of blessings."

"Can you believe I have a son," Michael said in the hospital as he held Edward for the very first time.

"I can, I certainly can," said Bea with tears in her eyes.

At home, the new brother and sister bonded well in the beginning. Then the slight jealousy came that often surfaced with a second child. Frances Elizabeth did not say much, but Michael and Bea could see the change.

"Frances Elizabeth, would you like to hold your little brother?" Bea asked. Frances Elizabeth had been asking to hold Edward every day since he had come home. She had a disappointed look when Bea asked her if she wanted to hold Edward.

"I think he's wet," she said in her little toddler's voice.

"Wet?" Bea said while checking Edward's diaper. "He's not wet."

"He don't like me Mommy," said Frances Elizabeth, still learning correct English.

"Yes, he does," said Bea. "I see the way he looks at you. You are his big sister. Come on over her and see his smile."

Bea played with Edward and said, "You like your big sister, don't you Edward?" Edward smiled and laughed. Frances Elizabeth joined in on the playtime and soon laughed.

"He's laughing," said Frances Elizabeth.

"I told you he likes you, sweetheart. He actually loves his big sister. And don't you ever forget that."

Bea had been able to aid the bonding process between Frances Elizabeth and Edward. The two children grew closer and closer with the days and months that passed and Frances Elizabeth was very protective of her little brother. As time went on, he too became very protective of her.

The next child to be born into the Peele Family was William Algernon Peele, in 1979, and was closely followed by Gerald "Thomas" in 1980. William and Thomas were so close in age that many people thought they were twins, even into adult life. They would even try to play little tricks on people sometimes but because one was taller most people learned to distinguish them apart.

"Tammy" Deniece Peele, a second girl, was born in 1983. She was strong willed even as a baby. With a big sister and three big brothers she always thought she could do anything they did. She was indeed a handful, and Bea had to keep a close watch on her. She crawled faster than any of the other children had and could be out of sight in a moment's time. But she soon learned to get in line with the others because Bea was not going to let her have control.

"Let her be," Michael would sometimes say in an effort to let Little Tammy have her way.

"Love her but do not spoil her rotten, Michael," Bea would often say. "No one will want to be around her if she is spoiled rotten child that grows up to be a spoiled rotten adult."

"She's a good girl, Bea."

"Michael, she needs discipline. She is a child and has to learn her place. Our job as her parents is to make sure that happens."

People often complimented Michael and Bea on the children's manners and behavior. Bea was a strong disciplinarian and worked hard to ensure that her children were polite and respectful to each other as well as to other people. Being a mother was Bea's most important position in life. She was very proud of her children and could always find a kind word of encouragement for each of them at any time of the day. She wanted to make sure she set good examples for them to follow.

"Mommy, tell Thomas I am his big brother," said William as he ran into the kitchen one Saturday morning when Bea was cooking breakfast. William was older but Thomas was taller. Thomas ran in the kitchen right after William. William was seven and Thomas was six.

"What's going on between you two?" said Bea.

"Tell him, Mommy. Tell him I'm the big brother," pleaded William.

"Look, Mommy," said Thomas. "I'm bigger than he is."

"William pushed Thomas away. "Get away from me. You're the little brother. Tell him, Mommy."

"Not another word," said Bea. "Go in the family room and sit on the couch. I will be in shortly." She looked back and forth between the two of them. "Not one word."

Bea turned the oven down low so the food would not burn. She walked toward the family room not knowing what she would say but gathering her thoughts with each step.

"Mommy," said Thomas.

"Not one word," said Bea.

She looked at William, then at Thomas, then again at each of the boys. Then she began to talk. "When I was a little girl I played with the neighborhood children and we had a lot of fun. Some of them were my cousins. But when it was time to go home we each went our separate homes. Most of the children in the neighborhood had at least one bother or sister, but not me. I went home alone. I longed for a little brother or sister but I was my mother's only child."

"But Mommy, I thought Aunt Janet was your sister," said William. "We call her Aunt Janet."

"Aunt Janet is my sister in so many loving ways," said Bea. But we grew up in different families. Aunt Janet and I became sisters as because we became such close friends."

"You didn't play with her as a little girl?" said Thomas.

"No baby," said Bea. "We became sisters as adults, after we both had children of our own."

"What about Aunt Ivy?" William said.

"Aunt Ivy is Daddy's sister. She grew up with Daddy. We became sisters after Daddy and I were married."

"What about Aunt Sylvia?" Thomas said.

"Aunt Sylvia is my natural sister. We have the same father but not the same mother. Aunt Sylvia is much younger than I am and she grew up in New York, so we didn't play together as children."

In the midst of the conversation the boys had forgotten all about why they were arguing.

"Mommy, that's sad that you had to grow up by yourself," said William. "Did you get scared?"

"Sometimes I did," Bea said.

"Wow, Mommy," said Thomas. "How did you do it?"

"It's a mystery and a miracle," said Bea with a sad look on her face.

Both boys fell into their mother's arms and she began to cry. "I have always felt that I missed so much by not having another child grow up with me," Bea said as she tightly held William and Thomas. "I guess that's why I have all five of you."

"Mommy?" Thomas pulled away to look in his mother's face. "Who is the 'big' brother?"

"Well Thomas, I look to William as your big brother, because he was born first, and he is a little wiser than you. And I expect him to be a good big brother and to protect. William is a big brother to you and to Tammy. But you are indeed a big brother to Tammy and I expect you to protect her. Do you think you can do that?"

"I do Mommy, I do. I think I can be a good big brother."

"Excellent, Thomas," said Bea with a big smile on her face. "Mommy will be watching you to make sure you are being a good big brother."

Chapter 5

In 1983, about three years after Tammy was born, Michael and Bea had another girl. She was named Dominique Cornelia Peele. She had a grand entrance into the world. She was an easy delivery, and she was a quiet, independent baby. She played by herself with ease. She was a very small child, but she sure did have a lot of energy. She seemed to do everything sooner than any of the other children. The other children took their first steps between nine and twelve months and were walking well between fourteen and fifteen months. Dominique took her first steps before she was eight months and she was walking at twelve months. She was exceptionally bright and loved to stay clean. She was Bea's little princess. Dominique was never a showy little girl. She had a kind and humble presence. And she loved her family. Her older siblings did not want her around at times because they were much older than she was. She was gracious even during those times when her siblings had other things to do.

"I am leaving for work," said Bea one Saturday morning as she headed to the hospital for a her seven a.m. shift. "Do not leave Dominique her by herself."

Bea did not hear a sound. Dominique was the youngest and only seven at the time.

"Is anyone listening? I said do not leave Dominique here by herself."

"We won't Mom," said Frances Elizabeth, twenty-three, who was visiting her family for the weekend but planning to get with her friends for the day.

"I hear you Mom," said Edward, who was twenty and attending Christopher Newport University, and had a Saturday job.

"Can anyone else hear me?" said Bea.

"We hear you Mom," said two voices simultaneously.

"Who is we? Is that William and Thomas?"

"Yes," said Thomas, fifteen at the time.

"Yes," said William, now sixteen.

"And do not leave Tammy to babysit Dominique. I mean that."

They knew Bea meant business. They just had to get their act together or they would be sorry for sure. When they all got together to discuss who would stay with Dominique everybody had plans. Even twelve-year-old Tammy was planning to meet with a group of girls at the library. One of the parents was going to pick them all up and wait with them at the library.

"I'm not afraid," said Dominique. "But I know Mommy will be mad if you leave me here alone. You can take me next door to Mrs.

Annie's house if she's not busy. She likes it when I come over, and I help her with things."

And that is exactly what happened. They called Mrs. Annie and she said she would love to have Dominique come over while they went to work and ran their errands. It was the one place Bea was comfortable with the older siblings leaving Tammy or Dominique.

The number of children was now six, three boys and three girls. They were a very close-knit family, especially as the children grew and matured. It was remarkable the way they cared for and supported each other. The year was 1996 and the older three children were out of the house and working, two were in high school, one in middle and one in elementary school.

Michael and Bea called a family meeting to make an announcement to their children. The children were somewhat nervous because they thought one of their parents might be ill. The announcement was that Bea was pregnant and due in January. Johnathan Devon Peele was born on Saturday, January 4, 1997. When they thought their family was complete they had a brand new "bouncing baby boy." The oldest child, Frances Elizabeth was twenty-five, old enough to have a child of her own, and the youngest, Dominique, was nine. Dominique became the best little mother's helper to Johnathan, and the other children took care of their baby brother from time to time.

Michael and Bea now had four boys and three girls. But tragedy struck this close-knit family when their father, Michael, died in a dreadful automobile accident in 2000. Michael was fifty-two. Bea was forty-eight with three children still at home, Tammy,

Dominique, and little Johnathan. The children all joined together to support each other and to help their mother get through this difficult time.

Frances Elizabeth got a job transfer back to the local area and moved in with her younger brother Edward. Everyone was working together to do whatever it took to make things more manageable for their mother. They made sacrifices to contribute financially so their mother Bea could take a much-needed break and they could all be in close proximity of their mother and each other. Although Dominique was only twelve she was already like a little mother to Johnathan. All the children worked well together and weathered that untimely storm.

"I could not believe it had happened," said Bea after a Saturday dinner when the entire family had gathered at Bea's home to remember Michael one year after he died. "I simply could not function. All of you stepped in and kept me going. I thank God for giving us Michael for the time we had him. I also thank each of you for the way you stepped in to keep this family together. I don't know what state I would be in today without your actions a year ago. Thank you all so very much."

Each family member was overwhelmed with emotion, but they were also being healed through being together.

"As the oldest child I felt a need to move back to the area to be with all of you," said Frances Elizabeth. "Not just for all of you but for me as well. I still miss Daddy a lot."

"As the oldest son Dad expected a lot from me," said Edward. "I didn't always come through, but when I did he let me know in a most profound way. I miss him."

At family meetings the children generally spoke in birth order, but sometimes Thomas would speak before William and then have to be told that it was not his turn. This day he patiently waited for William to speak.

"It's hard not having Dad here with us. I miss him too," said William. "I didn't realize how much I needed him. He took me on my first hunting trip. It was just the two of us. I felt so proud when we ate the venison for dinner the night after our successful hunting trip. I felt that I had become a man."

There was a long quiet pause after each child spoke. Everyone looked at Thomas, who always had something to say and sometimes had trouble waiting for his turn to say it. He lowered his head then looked up at his mother. His eyes were full of water. Bea smiled at him, and he composed himself.

"Dad was a good man," said Thomas. "He took me on my first fishing trip. I hadn't caught one fish and he had caught four. He said to me, 'Thomas, come over here and take this line.' The fish I pulled in was bigger than any of the fish he had caught so far. Dad said, 'Now you've got the idea.' I caught eleven fish that day. I was so happy."

"Daddy worked a lot of overtime," said Tammy. "But he always found time to help us with the important things in our lives. He was a strong man. Sometimes I was busy being a tomboy and trying to show up the guys. I hope I find a strong man like Daddy one day."

"Daddy used to dance with me," said Dominique. She stopped and cried softly. She was the youngest child in the family and used to love getting her Daddy, and anyone else, a cold glass of water. Michael often remarked that being a servant was one of Dominique's gifts. She was only twelve when Michael died. Everyone stayed quiet while Dominique cried softly. After a short while she continued. "Mom said I was Daddy's little princess. Daddy would say, 'Come, Little Princess and dance with the King.'" She stopped again, tears now running uncontrollably down her face. "I would put my feet on top of Daddy's and I would dance with him. I felt like a true princess. I was dancing with the King." She ran across the room and fell into her mother's arms.

Johnathan, now four, had started to cry because Dominque was crying.

"Johnathan," said Frances Elizabeth, who was holding Johnathan. "Do you remember Daddy?"

"Daddy," said Johnathan with a big smile on his face. He was pointing to a nearby picture of Michael.

It has been an emotional time for the Peele Family, but miraculously they made it through the day and each person was stronger because of the love and commitment they had for each other, love and commitment that started years ago with Michael and Bea. The family would laugh again and they would cry again as loving family members.

Chapter 6

Dominique was thinking about some of the Peele Family traditions when she thought about her brother Thomas, who usually left one of his Christmas trees up year around. One of his trees had stayed up for at least five consecutive years and most people loved it. Some family members and friends used Thomas's Christmas tree as an affectionate way of getting to his house just to hang out.

Something was always going on at Thomas's and Len. They were excellent hosts, never turning away anyone. The crowds of people that gathered regularly never seemed to bother or interrupt Thomas and Len's schedule. Whether it was food or conversation, they were generally ready to prepare and serve. They were used to feeding groups of people on their farm and they loved the feeding and the farming. Most of the other children had had enough of farming after being in the farming business with their father for most of their childhood.

Farming can be physically intense work, but Thomas loved it and he turned Len into a regular organic-growing, bee-keeping country girl. They worked so hard that it was easy to leave their

Christmas tree up throughout the year. It was the only way they could enjoy the beauty of the decorations themselves. They were too busy doing other things after they decorated the farm to enjoy the results of their labor. Yes, they decorated the farm. He had a special storage unit just for Christmas decorations and he was already behind the curve if he had not started decorating by the first of November. People came from miles around to see the "new stuff."

"Hey, come on up," Thomas would say if someone stopped by. He would stop what he was doing to show care and concern for others. One of his good friends, Charles, came up one cold Saturday morning to see the progress.

"I heard that you had some new decorations on the property. I thought I would take a look," said Charles, who came by for something at least once a week. Everybody loved hanging out with Thomas. He made you feel like he cared more about you than any other person on earth. That was Thomas.

"Come on in and get a cup of coffee and warm yourself first," said Thomas.

"I'm not staying Thomas, I know you're busy"

"Never too busy for a friend, come on in."

Charles followed Thomas into the house. The aroma of the coffee decorated the air.

"That smells delicious," said Charles.

"I hope it satisfies your tastes buds," said Thomas.

"I'm sure it will."

The two men sat and had coffee and for forty minutes. Thomas knew he had things to do, but work was never more important to him than family and friends. The decorations weren't going anywhere. They would be right there in that storage unit until Thomas was ready to continue putting them up. He took time and enjoyed a visit from his friend.

Charles was about to depart Thomas's company and the farm when he realized that he had not seen Thomas's new additions of Christmas decorations. Walking toward his car, Charles thought that he would have seemed rude to take up any more of Thomas's time. He decided to put a little spiral on his own plans.

"Thomas, what do you say I stick around awhile? I can get a glimpse of the new decorations while I help you put up some of the one in the storage unit," Charles said with a big smile on his face.

"I couldn't let you do that Charles. I'm sure you had some other plans."

"Forget those plans. Let do this."

"Okay," said Thomas. "Now I don't want to hear any complaining at church tomorrow about how hard I worked you."

"I won't complain, buddy. And don't you feel bad after I work circles around you today with these decorations."

They laughed and headed toward the storage unit. They were ready to continue their conversations and work on beautifying the grounds of the farm. The two friends bonded like inseparable brothers.

*****

One Saturday morning in mid-July Dominique was on one of her Christmas music thrills. She played Christmas music any day of the year. She even left a Christmas CD in the player in her car. Dominique delayed getting her car serviced because she did not want to take everything out of her car, especially her Christmas CDs. She would invariably misplace a favorite Christmas CD and have to grab a different one. She was full of miraculous beliefs, many of which might have seemed silly and meaningless to some people.

That was really all of the Peele family members. The Peele family was seriously engaged in fully celebrating Christmas, and celebrated at every opportunity—and they did get many opportunities. They always had room for a bit of Christmas. Any little thing would get them started and in the Christmas celebration mode. Even a simple phone call would be labeled a miracle and was enough to get them excited.

Dominique was getting ready to go grocery shopping when her cell phone rang. She did not recognize the number but decided to answer anyway.

"Domi?"

"May I ask whom you are trying to reach?" Dominique asked as she walked back toward her car.

"I'm trying to reach Dominique Cornelia Peele. Is this her number?"

And who may I ask is calling?" she asked as she quickly got into her car and closed the door for some privacy.

"This is Johnathan. Who is this?"

"This is Dominique, and what do you want? Whose number are you calling from and why are you calling me Domi?"

"I don't know. I thought maybe I had a wrong number. Sometimes Mom and Aunt Leta call you Domi calls."

"You're not Mom and you are not Aunt Leta. I'm in college now. I am not a little girl."

"Mom says you are Daddy's little princess."

"Johnathan, what do you want?" she asked, pausing after each word. "And whose phone are you using?"

"Okay, Dominique," he said her name slowly, pronouncing and holding each syllable for much too long. "I am in a store."

"For real. What do you want?" she asked. "I need milk and I want to get in and out of the store and get home."

"Anyway, I am in that little boutique on Main Street, Sway's Place. I see that necklace you wanted to get Mom for Christmas."

"The one with the heart-shaped locket?"

"Yes, Dominique. That would be the one." He said her name even slower this time.

"Are you sure it's the one?"

"It looks like the one you and Cousin Oveta were looking at. Why don't you come and see for yourself?"

"Okay, I'll be right there. Don't leave." She started her car.

"I've got some things to do too," said Johnathan.

"Johnathan, please don't leave." Her voice had softened by this time. She had been looking for that necklace for months.

"Okay, but don't be long."

"It's a miracle. Thank you Johnathan, I won't be long."

Dominique pulled out of the parking lot and in a short time was on Highway 17 headed north to a cute little boutique that had a little bit of everything, including some very elegant pieces of jewelry that her mother often commented on. Dominique was able to get the necklace for her mother's Christmas gift. She tucked it away in her little apartment in her bedroom dresser.

Chapter 7

Dominique was a young medical student who was completing a residency in Gloucester, Virginia. She had decided to reside in the local small town of Hayes. Her mother had lived in this town for a few years when her grandfather was in the military. Bea had graduated from Gloucester High School in 1970. Dominique wanted a quiet, peaceful place to call home when she was away from the busy life of a medical resident student.

"Oh, the joy of a peaceful home," she would often say as she entered her small, comfortable dwelling. "There is truly no place like home."

Dominique's time was an important resource and she had to carefully utilize every moment. She missed many meals because she was so engrossed in what she was doing that she didn't stop to eat. Some of her male cousins used to tell her she wouldn't find them too busy to miss meals.

Even with Dominique's active life she was never too busy to help her family and friends. Her many acts of kindness were attributes in her daily life. If she was doing something too pressing and the need for her time was not too serious she would offer her services for later. She didn't want people to think that they could take advantage of kindness, whether family or friend. Of course, one or two would always try to push her to the limit. She learned who those people were over time.

When Dominique was a young undergraduate away on her own for the first time she tried to help everyone. She later realized that as an unsuspecting teenager in college other students tried to benefit from her innocence and inexperience. It did not take her long to catch on the "games people play."

"I will kindly have to decline this time," she would say when she thought she might be treated unfairly or even if she felt there was a moderate likelihood that someone would take advantage of her.

One such incident happened in Dominique's first semester of college at Old Dominion University in Norfolk, Virginia. A student on her floor, Rebecca Lee, asked if she could borrow twenty dollars. Dominique had seen the young lady in the Perry Library studying and had also seen her in one of her rather large introductory classes. She decided to help the fellow student. Besides, the young lady said she needed the money to replace a very important textbook that had been stolen from her. The student seemed sincere and Dominique had, after all, seen her studying on more than one occasion. The student said she had most of the money, but needed just twenty more dollars. *What harm could it do?* She said she would pay Dominique as soon as she received a correspondence from her parents containing a check for two hundred dollars.

"Thank you so much, Dominique," Rebecca said. "I should get my check within the next few days."

"Sure, that's fine," said Dominique.

"I think I'll see if I can catch the bookstore before it closes."

"You don't have much time."

"Okay, see you later," said Rebecca. And she was on her way. Dominique generally kept a little cash on hand and felt happy about being able to help a fellow student. She felt hurt later when she found out that Rebecca had pulled that same rip-off scam on several other freshmen. She decided to get to know people better before loaning them her scarce and insufficient funds. She never saw that money again. And Rebecca Lee, well, she distanced herself from Dominique when she heard that Dominique was on to her scams. Dominique did not mind helping people, she actually enjoyed helping others, but she was certainly not going to let people continue to take advantage of her. She counted it a blessing and a miracle that Rebecca did not get more than twenty dollars.

Chapter 8

Dominique loved learning, which is why she work hard so hard in college and completed her undergraduate degree with honors. She was a Summa Cum Laude graduate with a 3.96 grade point average. Dominique was often referred to as a "bookworm." She had said that she just studied long hours and that other students could do the same. Many of them felt that if they studied twenty-four hours a day, seven days a week, they still could not have the grades Dominique had.

"Dominique, I really wish I could get good grades like you," Pamela said one afternoon after a Summer Undergraduate Research Fellowship project.

"Your grades are great," said Dominique.

"I should not even be in this program," said Pamela.

"Why would you say that?"

"Because it's true. You are really smart. But the only reason I'm here is because of my father's money."

"Really? Is that what you think?"

"Yes. And it's true. I don't even like what I'm doing."

"Are you serious?"

"Yes, I'm serious."

"Do your parents know how you feel?"

"Of course not. My parents would have a fit if they knew, especially my dad. Oh, Dominique, please don't tell anyone. Promise me you won't."

"I won't tell anyone Pamela, not as long as we are both here. I don't know what the future holds so I won't commit to any longer than that. I do think it would be wise for you to have a talk with you parents. Let them know how you feel. They'll understand."

"No they won't. My brother Anthony thought they would understand when he said he wanted to change his major to music. He loves music and he was pretty good with instruments and singing. My father said that if he wanted to major in music instead of engineering he might as well get out on the streets right now and learn how to take care of himself on pennies."

"What did your brother do?"

"He left and went to England. I haven't seen him in two years. My parents don't want me to even talk about him. They said he is a disgrace to our family."

"That seems kind of harsh."

"It is harsh, and I miss him so much. I worry about him, too. He is a good person. I don't understand how my parents could do that to him. He doesn't deserve that kind of treatment from anyone, especially parents."

"I can't tell you what to do Pamela, but I certainly will pray for you. That's a tough predicament to be in. I have such a close relationship with my mother. The thought of you not being able to share your innermost desires and thoughts with your mother saddens me. My mother always listens to me. She's the best."

"I am sad every day Dominique. I don't know how much longer I can do this. My grades are beginning to slip and Daddy said he simply would not pay for me to get poor grades. I'm doing everything I can to keep my grades up. There are just not enough hours in the day. I am tired, I am just so tired."

Pamela began to cry. Dominique didn't know what to say to her. She was sad that Pamela did not have evidence of a support system. Clearing her throat, Dominique gained enough courage to speak.

"How about talking with another family member, an aunt, an uncle, or a cousin? Maybe they could talk to your parents."

"You don't understand. I have crazy parents. The whole world thinks they're wonderful, with the exception of their two children."

The two young ladies stared at each other. They were motionless for a moment. Then Pamela broke the silence.

"I've already said too much. I need to leave. Please don't share any of this with anyone."

Pamela left in a hurry. Dominique did not know what Pamela was talking about, but something seemed terribly wrong. It was as if Pamela had shared some big family secret, but Dominique had no idea what Pamela was talking about.

Dominique went to her college dormitory room and tried to rest, but she couldn't. She got up and went to Pamela's room. Pamela was not there. Dominique was concerned so she went back to her own room and called her mother.

"Mom?"

"Dominique?" Bea said sensing concern in her daughter voice. "Are you okay?"

"I don't know. I think a classmate thinks she told me something secretive, but I have no idea what it could be."

"Dominique, what are you talking about?"

"I don't know. I guess I'm just tired."

"Are you in your room?"

"Yes."

"Is a resident assistant on duty?"

"I don't think so. I'm okay Mom, just jumping to conclusions."

"Conclusions about what? What's going on?"

Dominique wished she hadn't called her mother. Now her mother was concerned, and Pamela would think Dominique had broken her confidence. What was Dominique to do?

"I'm fine, Mom. Let me just get in these books and focus."

"Are you sure?"

"Yes, I'm sure."

"Now, don't you stay up too late," said Bea.

"I won't."

"I love you, Princess."

"I love you too, Mom."

Dominique said a prayer for her mother, for Pamela, and also for herself. So many things were proving to be distractors but Dominique knew she must stay focused. Her destiny depended on her ability to think quickly and to stay focused.

*****

Bea's baby girl was growing up much too fast, but this was yet another opportunity for Bea to put her trust in Dominique into action. Would her baby girl continue to pass these critical tests in life for which no textbook could ever prepare her? Bea said a prayer for Dominique and for Pamela.

Chapter 9

Dominique did not see much of Pamela after that night in which Pamela confessed that she had shared too much personal information. Pamela had already distanced herself from most students at school before that mysterious night. Dominique was on the verge of panic so she called her mother, who was not only her mother but also her friend and confidant. Pamela had distanced herself even from Dominique. Dominique prayed that Pamela would be able to talk with someone about whatever was going on in her life. Dominique knew that she didn't know the bigger picture, but God did. One day the two young ladies came face to face in the college cafeteria.

"Hello Pamela," Dominique said.

"Hello," said Pamela, looking away a split second after their eyes met. The dull sound in her voice spoke volumes about her displeasure in her obligation to return a greeting.

"Would you like to join me for lunch?" Dominique asked, wanting an opportunity to have some dialog with her classmate.

"No, not today, I have to study."

"Are you okay?"

"Yes, are you?" said Pamela, her tone hard and cold.

"Yes, I'm okay." Dominique said slowly and softly.

"Please stay away from me," Pamela said with a harsh sound in her voice that Dominique had never heard before.

"You don't mean that, do you?"

"I do mean that, Dominique. Why do you insist on annoying me? I don't want you in my life. You are a bother. Go away."

"Pamela, you don't mean that. Why are you doing this?"

"Doing what? Get a life will you, and leave mine alone."

"I will never give up on you," Dominique said.

"Why not, I've given up on you."

Dominique was perplexed. Pamela had opened up so freely at one point, and now she was unkind and unreachable.

Who was this person who had turned from a hurting schoolgirl to a cruel, heartless person? Dominique was at her wit's end with Pamela, and she just wanted to help. Pamela went from what seemed like being in fear to being ferocious in a short time frame. She disappeared from school of her own volition. Why could no one reach her? Why did she push everyone away?

One week later Dominique read in the local newspaper that Pamela was dead. The article said that she was found in her parents' bedroom lying peacefully on their bed, dead from a drug overdose.

*****

"Dominique, you need to move on," her mother said when she found Dominique sitting on the porch staring into outer space. Bea sat beside her daughter.

"I'm fine Mom."

"No you're not."

"I just wish there was something more I could have done."

"You did all you could, baby. You did all you could."

Dominique fell into her mother's arms and cried. She hadn't known Pamela very well, but she had enough information to know that Pamela was a young woman who was hurting and who felt scared and alone. Dominique had been trying to reach Pamela's brother, Anthony Forrest, for months. She wanted to share her concerns about Pamela with him. Dominique finally met Anthony at Pamela's funeral, and they exchanged phone numbers and met for coffee before he headed back to England. He blamed his parents for what happened to Pamela, and he wanted nothing to do with them. He stayed at a hotel while he was in the area for Pamela's funeral and didn't interact with either of his parents at the funeral.

Dominique stayed in contact with Anthony and tried to encourage him to make amends with his parents and to realize that they were also hurting. Many months later, with Dominique's coaching, Anthony said he was ready to face his parents, but he would only see them if Dominique went with him. When he came for the meeting Dominique joined him, and the meeting with his parents had a positive outcome. All three of them were hurting and agreed to make a new start. Dominique's patience and understanding had helped to open the door for healing and mending of broken hearts. As Dominique put it, it was a miracle.

*****

With time, Dominique finally moved on and submerged herself in her schoolwork. She graduated in the top five percent of her class at Old Dominion University with a bachelor's degree in physics. Dominique saw physics as being all about thinking and seeing things from a different perspective. She felt that her training in physics could be used for pretty much anything in life.

"Dominique, how did you get so smart?" said Michael Edward, Dominique's oldest brother, called Edward by family members.

"From my dear mother and through majoring in physics," said Dominique.

They laughed, both knowing their mother was witty and knowledgeable and that physics had taught Dominique so much but not nearly as much as her mother did.

"Did anybody else help you to get smart?" said Edward.

"Of course," said Dominique. "Every one of my siblings."

"Now you're talking," said "William" Algernon, the third child and the second oldest of the boys, who walked into the conversation just in time to get his "two-cents" worth on the table.

"Everybody has contributed to my education and growth," said Dominique. "And I appreciate all of it. Thank you very much."

The boys laughed. She knew they all loved their little sister, and each of them was protective of her in their own special way, even Johnathan, the youngest child.

"I don't know what's going on, but if Dominique is giving out a 'thank you' or two, count me in," said Johnathan walking in as Dominique said "Thank you very much."

"It's the little brother," said William. "He's lurking around to see what he can find out."

"Hey," said Johnathan. "I'm not so little anymore."

"You're right," said Edward. "But even though you're big, you're still the little brother."

Chapter 10

Most of the college students were in the dorms about mid-August. The new freshmen came early with their parents and lots of items they would not have time to use or wear. The minds of the returning students were back on campus life and their studies. They were happy to be back on their own. The newbie freshmen were endeavoring to settle in and get used to their new surroundings.

"I don't think you'll need this gown," a woman said to a young lady.

"You never know Mom. I want to be ready for everything."

"I want you to be ready to keep your grades up. This is a big sacrifice for your father and me. We want you to focus on your studies, so you can graduate on time."

"I will Mom, I will," she said looking all around and watching people her age walk around the campus. "I wish we had gotten here sooner. I feel like I'm late."

"That's what happens on a long drive with heavy traffic, dear."

"I know. I just want to get my things in my room so you and dad can get back on the road before it gets too late."

"Your father and I are staying for a parent orientation. We probably won't leave until tomorrow."

"Oh," said the young lady with a disappointed look on her face.

"Besides, we thought we would take you out to dinner tonight," said the mother.

"I'm good mom, I'm not even hungry."

"You need to eat something."

They kept talking as they walked toward the dormitory.

Dominique looked in disbelief. She was a light packer herself and did not bring a lot of fancy clothes, not even during her first year of college. She told her mother she would probably be sitting in her room most of the time. Dominique had never been big on the party scene, and she had not planned to start in college. She had done very well her first two years of college and wanted to keep her very respectable grade point average. She was now a resident assistant and had to be on campus early and in her assigned dorm to greet the newbies and assist them in getting settled. She was shocked to see the abundance of trunks and baggage some students brought. Where will they put it all?, Dominique was quite amused to watch some of the students struggle just to get their things out of their parents' vehicles. Most of the students were happy to be in college and out of their parents view. They seemed overjoyed and excited about their new life of freedom. Dominique smiled as she overheard two new freshmen chatting.

"Can you believe we're in college," the shorter of the two young ladies said.

"I think I'm dreaming and I don't want to wake up," the taller one said.

"I have never been so excited in my life."

"Neither have I."

Dominque listened as they walked with excitement, laughing and pointing at different people and buildings on the campus. Yes, they are newbies, and they probably have no idea the workload that is ahead of them, which needs to be completed neat and orderly and on time. That is, if they expect to graduate. The percentage of first year students that did not successfully complete their first year of college was high andwas gradually increasing.

Chapter 11

Dominique was living the busy life of an active college student, but she had certainly not forgotten the neighborhood children who admired her so much. They looked up to her and even had a little neighborhood talent show in her honor when she left for her first year of college. Dominique was not the best at everything, but she certainly did many things well. The children were always trying to impress her and the talent show was the way they showed their appreciation and thanked her for teaching their Sunday school classes and helping them in so many other ways.

"Miss Dominique," said Tanya one Sunday morning before Sunday school classes started. "Will you tell us about Jesus talking to the children and how He blessed them?"

Dominique had something different in mind that morning, but decided to put that on hold. The children loved to hear Dominique talk about how Jesus blessed the children because she demonstrated by selecting different children in the class and saying wonderful things about the children. Several parents had remarked about how it made the children feel so special.

"I think we might be able to do that today, especially since Jesus loves blessing the little children," said Dominique. "But before we start I will need everyone to get seated and quite."

As the children were getting settled, Dominique noticed that Jackson was not in the class. Jackson was from a broken home and did not always come to Sunday school. When he came he was frequently late. Dominique hoped he would be there because his little face lit up when she chose him for the demonstration about Jesus talking with the children and blessing them. The children were settled and Dominique had checked the attendance and prepared to begin, but Jackson still was not there.

"Okay, let's see who I will start with," said Dominique as she looked at each student and saw their excitement.

"Me, Miss Dominique."

"Me."

"No, me. Pick me."

"Pick me, I never get picked."

They were so full of excitement. But Dorothy Stewart did not raise her hand. She sat quietly at the table with her head hanging down. With all the excitement she just sat there daydreaming.

"Dorothy," said Dominique. "Are you okay?"

The other children raised their hands and asked to be selected but Dorothy did not say a word. She was in her own little world.

"Dorothy," said Dominique a bit louder this time and she kneeled in front of Dorothy.

Dorothy fell into Dominique's arms and fainted. Emergency medical help was called when a nurse in an adult Sunday school class had difficulty reviving Dorothy. After an examination at Gloucester Memorial Hospital doctors discovered that eight-year-old Dorothy had been traumatized due to a recent rape. The perpetrator was arrested a few days later. He was a family member who lived in the neighborhood.

Dominique spent countless hours by young Dorothy's side, in the hospital and at home, and she proved to be a vital part of Dorothy's road to recovery. That particular Sunday lesson had been put on hold, but God's love for children was still manifested and in His time He blessed each of the children.

"What at terrible thing to happen to a little girl," Bea said.

"Does Frances Elizabeth know?" Dominique asked.

"No, I don't think so. I don't have the heart to tell her," said Bea.

"Mom, someone needs to tell her."

"Oh Baby, talk to her. I don't think I can bear it."

A family member raped Frances Elizabeth's good friend, Ruth, when she was just a few years older than Dorothy. Frances Elizabeth had her own challenges as she grew to understand what had happened to her childhood friend. Ruth had not gotten over that stage of her life and still had counseling and psychiatric treatment as an adult. She never married and often closed herself off from the world. Together, Dominique and Bea told Frances Elizabeth the sad news about Dorothy. She handled it much better than they expected. She visited Dorothy and took her a stuffed animal.

Dominique had a unique was of reaching the heart of a person, especially young people. She would often sit and read to Dorothy. Days and weeks went by without a word from Dorothy. She just seemed to stare into space. Then one day as Dominique was reading she looked up from the pages of her book to the sight of a beautiful soft smile on Dorothy's face. She still did not say a word, but her smile said it all. She was miraculously improving. Dominique smiled back as a tear rolled gently down her cheek.

"Dominique, you are truly a change agent," said Frances Elizabeth. "You do the impossible to work with others to help others do the impossible. I am just amazed at the progress Dorothy has made. She is doing a wonder job of working and living on her own."

"It is truly amazing what love and patience will accomplish," said Dominique.

"I am so proud of Dorothy."

"And you should be. She is a remarkable little girl, she just needed a chance to prove it to herself and the world."

As with many others Dominique was loving and patient with Dorothy during those formative years of Dorothy's childhood and she helped Dorothy through many challenges. Dorothy told Dominique that she had become the single mentor who helped her to overcome the pain and stigma of being raped. At Dorothy's graduation celebration with family and friends, Dorothy recognized Dominique.

"I would like to ask my childhood neighbor, Dr. Jackson Clarke to join me," said Dorothy in the presence of many of her closest family members and friends.

Dr. Clarke joined Dorothy, now Dr. Dorothy Stewart.

"We would like to as Dr. Dominique Cornelia Peele to come forward at this time," said Dr. Jackson.

Dominique was surprised but stood and walked up to join them. She did not recognized Dr. Clarke until he said a few words.

"When I was a young boy I lived in this town," said Jackson. "I attended Gloucester Family Church and I loved Sunday school."

Dominique's eyes began to tear as she recognized Jackson from her Sunday school class.

"Miss Dominique was my Sunday School Teacher," continued Jackson. "I was from a dysfunctional family and when my parents refused to take care of me and left the area, I was sent to live with relatives in New Jersey."

"It's a miracle," said Dominique with tears streaming down her face. She was no longer able to contain herself. She had no idea what had happened to Jackson. The entire crowd was teary eyed.

"Last year I ran into Dr. Stewart at a conference in California for medical and mental health doctors," said Dr. Clarke.

"It's a miracle," said Dominique putting her wet face into her hands.

"Dr. Stewart and I had dinner one night and decided to do something special at her graduation celebration."

Dr. Stewart paused, then cleared her throat and took a deep breath.

"Today on behalf of the children at Gloucester Family Church, Dr. Stewart and I would like to present this plaque to Dr. Dominique Cornelia Peele. It reads, 'What would we have done without our favorite teacher and mentor?'"

"Thank you Miss Dominique," said Dorothy. "Thank you for believing in me." Dorothy hugged Dominique. There was not a dry eye to be seen.

Dominique was surprised and elated. She had continued to live a life of service to those around her and had seen the difference that love and patience made. She viewed many occurrences in life as miracles. Jackson had become a medical doctor and Dorothy had become a psychiatrist. They were miracles indeed.

Chapter 12

It seemed to Dominique like just a few weeks ago that Aunt Leta had been talking about the Christmas dinners at church that first Sunday in July. Now it was the end of November and Dominique was wondering what happened to August, September, and October. They were such a blur that Dominique had to stop and think about what she had accomplished. She was indeed a busy, proactive individual. Thanksgiving was over and it was time to focus a lot more on Christmas.

You have to be mentally ready for any event that the Peele Family is hosting, Dominique thought. *You might see your name on a program and not know how it got there, or you might be called on at the last minute to say or do something. Being ready is a characteristic that is expected in the Peele family.*

The Christmas dinners of 2014 turned out to be grand as usual. Aunt Leta was sort of in charge of all the dinners, even though she only hosted the Christmas Eve dinner. Each year she randomly asked someone to share a few words before dinner. She picked a person after they all gathered to bless the food. She warned the speaker that if they were too long she would stop them so everyone could eat. For the Christmas Eve dinner she would ask two people to say a few words. The second person was always chosen after the first one was finished. They also received the same warning. At the 2014 Christmas Eve dinner two family members had spoken and the person appointed to bless the food was about to pray when Aunt Leta said, "One more. Let's hear a few words from Dominique." This was different and unexpected.

Dominique had a strong voice for such a tiny person. As Aunt Leta put it, she was "a small piece of leather, but well put together." Aunt Leta did not repeat the warning, but Dominique knew she was standing between family and food.

"I will always believe in miracles," said Dominique. "I have experienced painful events in my own family, from the tragic automobile accident of my father to losing a job due to reorganization and budget cuts. I had to become like an eagle and learn to rise above it all and expect yet still another miracle.

"In my life I have experienced one miracle after another. Along the way there were times of challenges and times of pain, yet another miracle would always present itself. I often kept a smile on my face because no matter how hard life became or how painful my experiences were, I was always hopeful and expected another miracle. I have what I call a lot of 'Christmas Miracles.' Because the Peele Family celebrates Christmas all year long, I experience miracles all year long. Each job or assignment in which I find myself does not define me and is not the totality of who I am. It is just what I am doing at a given time before I go to heaven.

"Robert Kennedy once said, 'Tragedy is a tool for the living to gain wisdom, not a guide by which to live.' My mother said that the 'Bible is a guide by which to live.' We should learn to treat people with respect, kindness, and love. We never know what they are going through.

"Frances Elizabeth will you get my red purse? It is on Aunt Leta's bed."

Frances Elizabeth brought the purse to Dominique and she opened the purse and pulled out a small gift.

"My mother, Beatrice Walton Peele, has a heart of gold. She always told us that wherever you go and whatever you do, stay humble before the Lord and to keep Him in our heart. I would like to give her a special gift that I was saving for tomorrow."

Dominique took the gift to her mother and asked her to open it. It was the heart-shaped locket, with a picture of Bea on the left and a picture of Dominique on the right. Everyone clapped as Dominique graced her mother's neck with the precious gift.

"God is so faithful and so caring," said Dominique in closing. "He has given me many Christmas miracles, and He has a Christmas miracle just for you, if you will believe."

The food was blessed and the feast commenced. There were many more feasts and many more Christmas miracles in Dominique's life and in the Peele Family, but that one was special. It was her family's final Christmas with her mother Bea, who died unexpected in January, just days after Dominique's twenty-seventh birthday.

About the Bay Sisters

The Bay Sisters began in 2012 when Narielle Living, JM Johansen and Jackie Guidry joined together to write an anthology of Christmas Stories entitled *Chesapeake Bay Christmas*.

Jackie left the group when her husband was transferred out of state. Fortunately Gloria Savage-Early and Julie Leverenz decided to join our crazy family of writers.

This year, Gloria, Narielle, Julie and Jeanne (JM) are back with four new stories.

We are also fortunate to have photos from Julie Leverenz. In addition to being a writer, poet, photographer and all around great person, she is also a snow sculptor.

For more information, please visit their website at www.TheBaySisters.com.

JM Johansen

JM (Jeanne) Johansen was born in a small town in California. She and her brother grew up with a wild group of relatives – from

their Great Aunt Lura who was a Women's Temperance marcher with Carrie Nation to their crazy uncles who were never sober a day in their lives. Of course, she wrote about this in diaries she kept as a child.

She was the editor of her high school newspaper and has been a contributor to magazines over the years. Jeanne holds a Master's Degree in Health Care Administration. She is an award-winning author - in 2013 she was awarded second place in the Virginia state Golden Nib contest for fiction. Her first Novel – *27 Minutes-* detailed the struggle of homeless veterans. Her work has been published in several anthologies including *Chesapeake Bay Writers 20th Anniversary Anthology.* Her second book, *Chesapeake Bay Karma – the Amulet* (which she co-wrote) is available on Barnes and Nobel and Amazon.. She is a regular contributor to *Chesapeake Style Magazine.* She and her husband Carl live in Deltaville, Virginia. Visit her website at ***www.JeanneJohansen.com.***

Julie Leverenz

Julie Leverenz, writer and photographer, has won Firsts in the Virginia Writers Club Golden Nib contest (nonfiction), VWC

 Summer Shorts (fiction) and the York County Library Juried Literary Competition (poetry). Her essays and photos have appeared in the **Virginia Gazette** and the **Daily Press**. Julie also contributed a short story and a poem to the Chesapeake Bay Writers Anthology, **Harboring Secrets**. A New Jersey native, Julie earned degrees at Dickinson College and the College of William and Mary, where she founded the Women in Business Program. Julie lives in Virginia with her husband and a multi-talented cat. More information can be found at *www.julieleverenz.com*.

Narielle Living

Author Narielle Living spent her childhood in the small town of Watertown, CT, with a Virginian mother and Yankee father. School  spring breaks were spent driving to Richmond, VA for family visits, a torturous nine hours where she and her brothers pushed, shoved, whined and generally annoyed their parents. Once they got to Virginia, Narielle spent many hours trying to understand the Southern drawl and figure out what other kids were saying to her. Today, Narielle is a regularly featured writer for the Hampton Roads magazines Next Door Neighbor. Her mysteries, *Signs of the South* , *Past Unfinished, and Revenge of the Past and Chesapeake Bay Karma – The Amulet* are available through Amazon and Barnes & Noble. A former massage therapist, she also studied Philosophy and Religion. Narielle lives in southeastern Virginia and is currently working on her third and fourth books simultaneously. For additional information about her books, please visit her website at ***www.NarielleLiving.com.***

Gloria J. Savage-Early

Gloria J. Savage-Early is the Site Director for Old Dominion University. She is currently pursuing a Ph.D. The sixth of seven

 children born to Thomas and Beatrice Savage in North Carolina, she treasures her relationships with family and friends. She married her high school sweetheart, and they served together in the United States Air Force, where their son currently serves.

She is a member of the Association of University Administrators and Golden Key International Honor Society. She serves on several boards and recently gave the graduation address at Ware Academy.

She is a contributor to *Harboring Secrets*, the Chesapeake Bay Writers 20th Anniversary Anthology. She is a member of Chesapeake Bay Writers. For more information, visit her website at *www.GloriaJSavage.com.*

www.ingramcontent.com/pod-product-compliance
Lightning Source LLC
Chambersburg PA
CBHW070005260626
47159CB00005B/1669

* 9 7 8 0 9 8 8 4 6 3 7 3 8 *